# EZRA'S GAMBLE

## BY RYDER WINDHAM

*For Alan Harris, who is a much nicer fellow than Bossk.*
*—R.W.*

The Imperial propaganda recording in chapter two
is adapted from the *Star Wars* radio drama by Brian Daley.

This book's final chapter is adapted in part from the
*Star Wars Rebels* script "Not What You Think," by Simon Kinberg.

# EGMONT
*We bring stories to life*

First published in Great Britain 2014
by Egmont UK Limited, The Yellow Building,
1 Nicholas Road, London W11 4AN.

ISBN 978 1 4052 7576 7
59018/1
Printed in UK

Stay safe online. Any website addresses listed in this book are correct at the
time of going to print. However, Egmont is not responsible for content hosted by
third parties. Please be aware that online content can be subject to change
and websites can contain content that is unsuitable for children.
We advise that all children are supervised
when using the internet.

# CONTENTS

# CHAPTER 1
# THE **PICKPOCKET** AND THE **BOUNTY HUNTER**

'**Welcome** to Lothal, sir,' Ezra Bridger said to the tall male Chagrian who had just arrived at the spaceport with four female blue-skinned Twi'leks. 'Are you here for the big fight?'

'Fight? What fight?' said the Chagrian. The four Twi'leks came to a stop behind him. The Chagrian wore an expensive coat, and on the coat's collar was an Imperial allegiance pin. On his left hand, he wore a jewelled ring and a silver wrist-comm. He turned his long-horned head to face the spaceport concourse's security station, where two armoured stormtroopers stood, holding matching blaster rifles. Seeing that the stormtroopers were watching other travellers and not looking in the direction of his group, the Chagrian bent close to Ezra and said, 'Keep your voice down, boy. Is it true that a Houk will be fighting a Feeorin?'

'Yes, sir. A genuine gladiator match.'

'I need five seats. How much?'

'Five hundred credits, sir.'

'Five *hundred*?' Suspicious, the Chagrian looked Ezra up and down.

Ezra wore a backpack and a sleeveless jacket over ratty overalls and had a scavenged piece of armour over the shin of his right leg. He also had a retractable energy slingshot mounted to the gauntlet that was wrapped around his left wrist, but the Chagrian didn't notice the weapon.

The Chagrian said, 'Are you authorised to sell tickets?'

'Indeed I am, sir,' Ezra said. 'And I can offer you very good seats.' He reached into his backpack and removed a small datapad. He activated the datapad's imagecaster, and a three-dimensional hologram appeared in the air. The hologram showed a wide ring of seats that encircled a large cage. 'You'd be sitting there.' Ezra pointed to five seats that were only a few rows away from the cage. 'But for just another hundred credits, you and your lovely companions could have your own private box.' He smiled at the Twi'leks and winked at the tallest one. All four Twi'leks giggled, causing their head-tails to jiggle against their backs.

'Very well,' the Chagrian said. He reached for a pouch on his belt and removed six credit chips.

Taking the credit chips, Ezra said, 'Your pin looks dull.'

'I beg your pardon?'

'Your Imperial pin. It doesn't look like you polished it recently. The local authorities wouldn't approve.' Shifting the datapad so that he held it with one hand, he used his free hand to pull a clean rag from his jacket pocket. 'Here, use this.'

The Chagrian took the rag and began rubbing at the pin. Moving closer to the Chagrian, Ezra patted his sleeve and said, 'Oh, I forgot to mention. For an additional hundred credits, your box could have an all-you-can-eat buffet.'

The Chagrian handed the rag back to Ezra. 'Is the food good?'

'Yes, sir, the best on the planet.' He reached up to move the rag over the Chagrian's pin and said, 'Pardon me, sir, you missed a spot.'

The Chagrian gave Ezra another credit chip. Ezra tapped at the datapad, and a small card slid out of its side. Handing the card to the Chagrian, Ezra said, 'This is your group's ticket. Present it to the admissions office at Monad Outpost, and you'll be escorted to your private box, where your buffet will be waiting.'

'How do I get to Monad Outpost?'

'You'll need to take a shuttle, sir.'

The Chagrian rolled his eyes. 'And how much will *that* cost?'

'Forgive me, sir, I forgot to tell you. Because you purchased box seats, a complimentary public shuttle is waiting for you and your group at the spaceport's ground transport area. The shuttle is courtesy of the event's promoter.'

'That's very generous!' said the Chagrian.

Moving closer to the Chagrian, Ezra lowered his voice and continued, 'However, just so you're aware, you see that group over there?' He directed the Chagrian's gaze to several green-skinned Rodians who were having some difficulty instructing a droid to carry their luggage.

The Chagrian sneered. 'Rodians. Ugh! I can smell them from here.'

'Well, confidentially, they purchased tickets for box seats, too, and the public shuttle's driver is obligated to give them a ride, too. I hope you won't mind me saying this, sir, but I imagine a sophisticated gentleman such as yourself, and also your enchanting companions, would be far more comfortable in a private air taxi.'

The Twi'leks nodded in agreement. The Chagrian gave Ezra a sceptical glance and said, 'A private taxi, eh?'

'Fortunately for you, the finest taxi has not yet left the spaceport. The driver is a Bardottan. You'll find him at the ground transport area.' Ezra bowed politely and held out one hand, waiting for the Chagrian to give him a tip.

The Chagrian ignored Ezra's open hand and walked off, leading his Twi'lek companions past the spaceport's security checkpoint. The tallest Twi'lek glanced back at Ezra and winked at him, and then she moved past the checkpoint and Ezra lost sight of her on the crowded concourse.

Ezra smirked. Along with the credits that the Chagrian had given him, he had also managed to take the Chagrian's Imperial pin, jewelled ring, wrist-comm, and most of the contents from his money pouch. He bundled the loot into his rag and stuffed it into his backpack. He was about to scan for more wealthy-looking tourists when he saw a Xexto walking towards him.

The Xexto was Ferpil Wallaway, who owned a pawn shop on Lothal. He was also a skilled pickpocket and had various underworld connections. He had a small head with large dark eyes, a long, skinny neck, and six arms. In one of his free hands, he held a datapad that was identical to the one Ezra carried. An inexpensive chronometer was wrapped around another wrist. He stopped in front of Ezra and said, 'How's business?'

'I sold five more tickets,' Ezra said.

'Good.' Ferpil looked around to make sure no one else could hear him, then leant close to Ezra and said, 'I think Imperial spies may be watching us. Don't get caught lifting anything you shouldn't.'

'I won't,' Ezra said. 'You taught me every trick I know.'

'That may be,' Ferpil said. 'But I didn't teach you everything *I* know.' He took a step back, and Ezra noticed that in one hand, Ferpil held the rag-bundled credits and valuables.

Ezra sighed. 'Imperial spies, huh? How do you always manage to distract me before you pick me clean?'

'Because I'm very good at what I do,' Ferpil said as he removed the credit chips from the bundle. 'These chips go to the Commissioner. You'll receive your share after the fight.' He discreetly handed the remaining valuables back to Ezra and added, 'Bring this stuff and the datapad to my shop later, and I'll pay you what I can.'

'Fair enough,' Ezra said as he returned the stolen goods to his backpack. 'Just out of curiosity, has anyone actually seen the mysterious Commissioner, or figured out who he is?'

'Not that I'm aware,' Ferpil said. 'All I know is that he pays on time.'

'Speaking of time,' Ezra said, 'do you want this?' He reached into his jacket and pulled out Ferpil's chronometer.

Ferpil's dark eyes widened. 'Impressive!' His face broke into a wide smile as he took back his chronometer and clamped it around his wrist. 'See you later, Ezra.'

Ferpil walked off. Ezra surveyed another group of arrivals, examining their clothes to estimate their wealth. He was about to approach one group when a girl's voice called out, 'Hey, Ezra! Ezra Bridger!'

Ezra turned to see a red-haired girl standing in a long line with other people, waiting to board a medium-sized passenger ship that rested on a landing pad. The girl smiled at him and waved.

Ezra recognised Moreena Krai. Like him, she was fourteen years old. She stood beside her parents and younger sister, who had also turned to face Ezra. Moreena stepped out of line and walked quickly over to him.

Ezra said, 'What's going on?'

Moreena bit her lower lip. 'My family and I . . .

we're leaving.'

Ezra raised his eyebrows. 'Leaving? As in permanently?'

Moreena nodded. 'We're going to live with my grandmother. I tried to send a message to you, but . . . I'm sorry. Everything happened so fast.'

Ezra shook his head in disbelief. 'But what about your farm?'

'The farm's gone.' Moreena's gaze drifted to the stormtroopers at the security station. 'The Empire wanted the land to extend their mining operations.'

Ezra scowled. 'Did they pay your parents anything?'

'No. The Imperials just condemned the property and took it.'

Ezra shook his head. 'They've done it before, and there's no one to stop them. But farmers have found other ways to make a living on Lothal. Why did your parents decide to leave?'

'My parents aren't like us,' Moreena said. 'They remember what Lothal was like before the Empire. All they ever wanted was to live on their own farm. But after Palpatine became Emperor, and the Empire took over Lothal, and . . . well, so much has changed. . . . We just can't live here anymore.'

Ezra saw tears welling up in Moreena's eyes. He

grimaced and said, 'I'm sorry.'

Moreena brushed away a tear. 'It's not your fault.'

'I know,' Ezra said. Lowering his voice, he added, 'But don't mind me if I do my best to kick every stormtrooper off this planet.'

'That could take a lot of kicking.'

Ezra pointed to his right leg and said, 'I'm already wearing my shin guard.'

Moreena laughed. 'So, what brings *you* to the spaceport?'

'There's a sporting event tonight. A big fight between gladiators. Things like that attract people with money. And you know what people with money attract?'

'You.'

'Yeah, but don't tell everyone, or they'll be jealous.' Ezra's eyes became suddenly glued to a female Balosar tourist who wore a broad shimmersilk scarf wrapped delicately around the two antennapalps that extended from the top of her head. Ezra muttered, 'That scarf's got to be worth at least a thousand.'

Moreena's father called out, 'Come on, Mo! Get back in line!'

'Just a moment,' Moreena called back. 'Ezra, can I ask you something?'

'Hmmm?' Ezra tore his gaze from the Balosar's

scarf. 'Sure, ask away.'

'Have you ever thought about leaving Lothal?'

'Me? Leave?' Ezra chuckled. 'And let someone else have all the fun of ripping off Imperial idiots?'

Moreena sighed. 'I don't understand. There's nothing keeping you here. And it makes me so sad, thinking of you all alone, without your parents. I wish –' She stopped talking.

At the mention of Ezra's parents, his expression turned grim. 'Don't, Moreena,' he said. 'Don't ever feel sad for me. I've always done just fine on my own, and I always will.'

'Well, then. I guess this is goodbye. Take care, Ezra.' Moreena turned and began walking back to her family.

'Wait!' Ezra said. 'Where does your grandmother live?'

Moreena glanced back. 'Alderaan,' she said. Then she returned to the line.

Ezra watched Moreena and her family board the ship. As a group of travellers wearing Imperial pins walked by, he knew he was missing plenty of opportunities to obtain more money. But he continued to watch the ship as its repulsorlift engines fired, and then the ship lifted off the landing pad and ascended into the sky. Over the years, he'd seen many starships come and go, but as the passenger ship vanished into the clouds, he had a feeling that he wouldn't see that ship, or Moreena or her family, ever again.

A patrol of Imperial TIE fighters soared over the spaceport. Seeing the TIE fighters, Ezra Bridger let his thoughts drift to the small collection of stormtrooper helmets that he kept at home. He wondered if he'd ever get the chance to steal a TIE fighter pilot's helmet.

A bounty hunter's freighter dropped out of hyperspace and angled towards the planet Lothal. Inside was Bossk, a Trandoshan with greenish-yellow scales. His freighter was a modified Corellian Engineering Corporation YV-666 named *Hound's Tooth*, which had an elongated, rectangular hull and reinforced armour plating. From his seat in the cockpit on the command bridge, Bossk gazed at a monitor that displayed Lothal, a blue-and-green world with a cloudy atmosphere.

A light flashed on Bossk's control console as Imperial sensors scanned his ship. From the console's comlink, a voice said, 'Lothal Imperial Spaceport Authority to CEC YV-666. Identify yourself and state your business.'

The Trandoshan replied, 'My name's Bossk. I'm a licensed bounty hunter. My Imperial Peace-Keeping Certificate number is five-five-nine-four-six-one-one-two. There's a bounty on a Dug criminal, Gronson "Shifty" Takkaro, who jumped bail in the Ahakista system. I'm here to find and apprehend Shifty, and bring him back to Ahakista.'

'You're hunting Gronson Takkaro?'

Bossk gnashed his sharp teeth. 'Yes.'

'One moment,' said the Spaceport Authority agent. 'I'm transferring you to Imperial Security Bureau headquarters.'

Bossk waited for nearly thirty seconds before he heard a loud beep from his holocomm. A hologram appeared over his console, and he stared at the light-generated three-dimensional image of an Imperial officer with a neat haircut. The officer said, 'I've been informed that you're looking for Gronson Takkaro, a Dug criminal, on Lothal?'

'Correct,' Bossk said.

'Why are you looking for him?'

'The bounty was posted via the Imperial Enforcement DataCore. You should have all the info on file.'

'But I would appreciate it if you told me yourself,' the officer said testily.

Bossk gnashed his teeth again. 'Gronson Takkaro, generally known as Shifty, is a gambler and former operations manager of the Daystar Casino on Ahakista. He owes a lot of money to some very influential people, including an Imperial senator, Hack Fenlon. Senator Fenlon submitted the bounty, and he wants Shifty captured alive and returned to Ahakista.'

'You're certain that Shifty – I mean, Gronson Takkaro – is on Lothal?'

'I wouldn't be here if I weren't certain. He arrived on Lothal nine days ago, smuggled aboard a drone barge. I have datatapes to prove it.'

The officer was silent for a moment, then said, 'I recently received a report that a Dug gambler has been frequenting a business establishment in the city's northern sector. I shall send a detachment of stormtroopers to arrest him at once.'

Struggling not to sound outraged, Bossk said, 'With all due respect, officer . . . ?'

'Herdringer,' the officer said, sharply. '*Lieutenant* Herdringer.'

'Lieutenant Herdringer, the reason that Senator Fenlon placed a government bounty on Shifty is because Shifty already managed to elude Imperial authorities in three systems. Also, in case you didn't know, when the Bounty Hunters Guild assigns a hunter to pursue an acquisition who is the subject of a government bounty, only that particular hunter – in this case, myself – is authorised to go after that particular acquisition.'

'But –'

'Let me put it this way, Lieutenant,' Bossk interrupted. 'If I fail to get Shifty, that's not going to affect your career one bit. However, if your stormtroopers interfere with a government-approved bounty, and they fail to get Shifty . . . well, it wouldn't look good for you.'

'I see your point,' the officer said. 'But if the report that I received about the Dug is correct, he's in a civilian zone of the city. Can you avoid the use of firepower?'

Bossk snorted. 'I'm not getting paid to kill Shifty. I'm getting paid to bring him back to the Ahakista system *alive*.'

'Very well,' the officer said. 'The report indicates that the Dug was sighted at Ake's Tavern. I'll inform the Spaceport Authority that you have clearance to land, and provide a TIE fighter escort.'

Before Bossk could request the address for Ake's Tavern, or discourage an escort of TIE fighters, the hologram of the officer flickered and vanished. Bossk muttered to himself. The last thing he wanted was for any criminals to become aware of his arrival on Lothal, but a freighter with a TIE fighter escort would almost certainly attract some attention. As *Hound's Tooth*'s automatic pilot calculated a trajectory to the planet's surface, Bossk eased back into his seat and thought about his exchange with Lieutenant Herdringer. Although he didn't trust Imperials in general, his instincts told him that Herdringer was especially untrustworthy.

Bossk reached down beside his seat and picked up his mortar gun. He inspected the weapon and then inspected it again. "'Avoid the use of firepower,'" he said with a throaty chuckle. 'We'll see about that.'

# CHAPTER 2
# EZRA'S NEW JOB

**'You, too,** can be part of the Imperial family,' a recorded voice boomed from the speakers located above the spaceport's Imperial security station. 'Don't just dream about applying for the Academy, make it come true! You can find a career in space: Exploration, Starfleet, or Merchant Service. Choose from navigation, engineering, space medicine, contact/ liaison, and more! If you have the right stuff to take on the universe, and standardised examination scores that meet the requirements, dispatch your application to the Academy Screening Office, care of the Commandant, and join the ranks of the proud!'

Ezra Bridger had been continuing his work at the busy spaceport, and he easily ignored the Imperial propaganda recording as he placed more stolen items into his backpack. But he couldn't help hearing the screeches of TIE fighters as they circled back overhead. He looked skywards and spotted an unusual freighter descending towards a landing pad. By his eye, the freighter's long, angular hull resembled a large, blunt weapon.

Despite all the noise around and above the spaceport, Ezra also heard approaching footsteps. He stepped aside just in time to avoid being knocked over by a squad of stormtroopers who ran to the edge of the landing pad beneath the incoming freighter. He realised that the TIE fighters had escorted the freighter to the spaceport.

Blasts of steam from the freighter's thrusters kicked up dust as the ship touched down. Curious about who or what the freighter was carrying, Ezra walked closer to the landing pad but kept his distance from the stormtroopers who stood watching the freighter. He came to a stop beside some empty cargo containers.

A hatch opened at the back of the freighter, and a tall reptilian humanoid stepped out. Ezra recognised the alien as a Trandoshan. The Trandoshan wore an ill-fitting pressure suit that exposed his long muscular forearms and lower legs. His clawed feet were also bare. He carried a black mortar gun with an extended barrel and had ammunition cartridges wrapped around both legs, just below his knees.

One of the stormtroopers walked up to the Trandoshan and the two began talking. The Trandoshan dipped a claw into a pocket on his pressure suit and showed a datacard to the stormtrooper. The stormtrooper nodded, then turned and walked away from the landing pad. The other stormtroopers followed him.

Still standing by the cargo containers, Ezra watched the stormtroopers walk off, then looked back to the freighter. The Trandoshan had vanished. Ezra noticed that the freighter's hatch had sealed, and he wondered if the Trandoshan had returned to his ship. He took a cautious step forwards so he could have a wider view of the landing pad, but as he edged around the cargo containers, he found the Trandoshan standing in the shadows of the containers, facing him. The Trandoshan held his mortar gun at a low angle, its barrel casually pointed at Ezra's legs.

The Trandoshan hissed, 'Looking for something, shorty?'

'I was just admiring your ship, sir,' Ezra said.

'Don't admire it too closely. Its security system has a habit of blasting snoops.'

'I'm not a snoop, sir. I'm –'

'Keep your hands where I can see them,' the Trandoshan interrupted as his red eyes flicked to Ezra's left wrist. 'An energy slingshot. Cute.'

Ezra cleared his throat. 'Please allow me to introduce myself. Ezra Bridger, official guide to Lothal, at your service.' Ezra bowed.

The Trandoshan snorted. 'At my service? Kid, do you have any idea what line of work I'm in?'

'Well, I'm just guessing, sir,' Ezra said, 'but I couldn't help noticing that your ship is equipped with missile launchers as well as quad cannons, and that the Imperials seemed very interested in your arrival. And given the size of your mortar gun, and the way you don't mince words, it's my impression that you're a professional bounty hunter.'

'Maybe you're not as dumb as you look,' the Trandoshan said. He lowered his gun. 'I need to meet a guy at a joint called Ake's Tavern. Unfortunately, the Imperials weren't very interested in giving me directions.'

'Ake's Tavern is in the northern market district,' Ezra said, 'but it's kind of hard to find. I'd be happy to bring you there myself, Mr . . . ?'

'Bossk.'

'But I regret I'm somewhat busy at the moment. You see, I'm selling tickets for a major sporting event tonight, and I –'

'Get me to Ake's Tavern right now,' Bossk interrupted, 'and I'll pay you one hundred credits.'

Ezra said, 'I hope you won't think me difficult, but my time is worth more than that.'

'And my time is more valuable than yours. You'll get one *thousand* credits, and not one credit more, if we leave *now*.'

Ezra knew he'd be pushing his luck if he haggled further, but he said, 'Half up front?'

Bossk gave Ezra a chip worth five hundred credits. Ezra aimed a thumb in the direction of the spaceport's exit and said, 'Right this way, Bossk.'

'Watch your mouth, shorty,' Bossk said as he wagged a thick-clawed finger at Ezra. 'To you, I'm *Mr* Bossk.'

Inside a tall building that overlooked the spaceport, Lieutenant Jenkes, a grey-uniformed officer of the Imperial Security Bureau, stood before his office's wide window. From Jenkes's elevated vantage, the pedestrians at the spaceport were so far away that they appeared as small dots to the naked eye. But Jenkes was peering through macrobinoculars, and he could clearly see the Trandoshan who was being led by a dark-haired boy through a cluster of travellers and past the Imperial security checkpoint. Because Jenkes had observed the Transdoshan handing a credit chip to the boy, he suspected the Trandoshan had hired the boy, if only temporarily.

A loud electronic chirp sounded from a holocomm console behind Jenkes. He lowered his binoculars and turned to see a hologram of a stormtrooper materialise above the console. The stormtrooper said, 'TK-5331 at checkpoint five to Lieutenant Jenkes.'

'Report,' Jenkes said.

'The bounty hunter has left the spaceport, sir.'

'Dispatch Squad Five to keep an eye on him,' Jenkes said. 'His assignment has been approved by the Imperial Security Bureau, but only if he captures his target without the use of firepower. I won't tolerate any blaster fights within city limits.'

'Yes, sir,' said the stormtrooper, and then his hologram flickered and vanished.

Jenkes reached into a pocket on his grey tunic and removed his private comlink. He checked the comlink's controls to make sure the scrambler was activated so no one could record his transmission or trace it back to him. He keyed in a series of numbers and held the comlink close to his ear. A moment later, he heard a deep voice respond, 'Yes?'

Jenkes said, 'The bounty hunter has left the spaceport and is heading for your position. He may be accompanied by a boy with dark hair, wearing a backpack.'

The deep voice responded, 'You said Bossk would be alone.'

'I said he *usually* works alone.'

'Is the boy working with Bossk?'

'Possibly.'

'We never talked about a kid being involved.'

'The boy isn't my concern,' Jenkes said. 'I only mentioned him to help you spot Bossk.'

The speaker with the deep voice laughed. 'I don't think we'll have any trouble spotting a Trandoshan bounty hunter on Lothal. You want the kid blasted, too?'

Jenkes exhaled loudly through his nose. 'I said the boy isn't my concern. That means I don't care whether he lives or dies. But just so we're crystal clear on the situation, you're only getting paid to kill Bossk. Understood?'

'Understood,' said the deep voice without any indication of pleasure.

Jenkes broke the connection and put his comlink back in his pocket. He returned to his holocomm console and pressed a switch. The same stormtrooper that he'd spoken with earlier reappeared and said, 'TK-5331 here, sir.'

'Make sure Squad Five uses remotes as they follow the bounty hunter,' Jenkes said. 'If anything unexpected happens at Ake's Tavern, I want recordings.'

'Yes, sir.'

Jenkes switched off the holocomm and smiled. He was looking forward to watching the recordings.

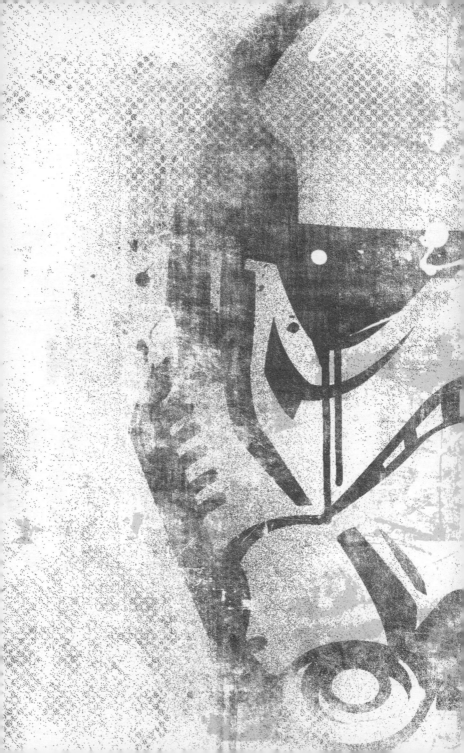

# CHAPTER 3
# AN **EXPLOSIVE** **CONFRONTATION**

**The civilian** speeder bus that Ezra and Bossk boarded after they left the spaceport was almost fully occupied, but all the other passengers shifted their positions and squeezed against each other to keep their distance from the tall Trandoshan and his menacing weapon. The bus was an express, with only one stop between the spaceport and Capital City's northern market district. When the bus came to the first stop and hovered alongside a building that had been closed ever since the Imperials arrived on Lothal, the droid who sat behind the bus's controls was surprised when almost all the passengers poured out at the same time, causing the bus to wobble in the air.

The droid rotated one mechanical eye to glance to the back of the bus and saw Bossk with his blaster standing beside Ezra. The droid said, 'Oh, dear.'

'Get moving, droid,' Bossk snarled.

The speeder bus lurched forwards. Ezra gestured to a row of empty seats and said, 'Would you like to relax your legs, Mr Bossk?'

'I'll relax when I'm dead.'

Ezra decided to remain standing too. He looked out a window. They were travelling so fast that the buildings and cross streets appeared as high-speed blurs. He said, 'We'll be at the final stop in about four minutes. Ake's Tavern is just a short walk from there.' He looked up at Bossk. 'Mr Bossk, did you say that you're meeting a friend at the tavern?'

'No. I said I was meeting a *guy*.'

'Is he a business associate? Or a client?'

'What's it to you?'

'Well, I've never been inside Ake's Tavern before, but I've heard from reliable sources that the service isn't always very good. If you and the, uh, guy that you're meeting are interested, I happen to know of another establishment that I'm certain you'd enjoy. It's a little bit more expensive, but –'

'You talk too much,' Bossk said.

Ezra remained silent for the rest of the ride.

The bus came to a stop at a terminal at the heart of the market district. Bossk stepped out of the bus first. Although the pavements were crammed with pedestrians shopping for food, clothing, and various goods approved by the Empire, everyone moved away from him.

Keeping his eyes on the crowd, Bossk said, 'Which way?'

Ezra pointed to a side street that was lined with small shops. Bossk started towards it. Ezra had to walk fast to keep up with the Trandoshan's long strides. Three Ugnaughts stepped out of one shop directly in front of Bossk.

Bossk snarled. The squat, porcine humanoids squealed and nearly stumbled over each other as they moved fast to get out of Bossk's path. One Ugnaught fell in front of Ezra, and Ezra jumped over him so he could catch up with Bossk. Ezra said, 'I've noticed that you have a way with people, Mr Bossk.'

Bossk shrugged. 'It's a gift.'

'Ake's Tavern is just around this corner, at the end of the block on the left,' Ezra said. But as he rounded the corner, he realised Bossk was no longer walking beside him. He doubled back and found Bossk standing still, looking in the direction of the departing Ugnaughts, as if he'd lost something. 'Mr Bossk? Is everything all right?'

Bossk shook his head. 'No. Everything is most definitely not all right.'

'What's wrong?'

Bossk faced Ezra. 'I forgot the name of the guy I'm supposed to meet.'

'Oh,' Ezra said. 'Well, do you think he'll recognise you?'

'Of course, he'll recognise me,' Bossk said. 'But that's not the point! In my line of work, if a hunter forgets something important, like a name, during a business meeting, that's an awful mistake. It's considered . . . unprofessional.'

'Oh,' Ezra said. 'I'm sorry you can't remember, but . . . Mr Bossk, I did bring you to Ake's Tavern, and I have other business elsewhere. You owe me five hundred credits, and –'

'How'd you like to earn an extra five hundred?'

'What?'

Bossk removed a credit chip from a pocket and gave it to Ezra. 'Here's the five hundred that I owed you. To earn the extra five hundred, all you gotta do is go inside the tavern and say, "Is someone here waiting for Mr Bossk?" Then the guy will probably wave at you, and you can ask for his name. After he tells you, you say, "Mr Bossk will be here in a moment." Then you come back outside, tell me the guy's name, and you'll get another five hundred. Deal?'

'Sounds easy enough,' Ezra said. 'But . . . I don't know. The way I figure it, I'm not just helping you out, I'm saving your professional reputation. And I've never been inside Ake's Tavern before. I mean, I'm only fourteen years old, and according to Imperial law, I shouldn't even go near a place like –'

'A thousand,' Bossk said. 'You'll get another thousand.'

Ezra grinned. 'Deal. Wait here. I'll be right back.'

Ezra walked around the corner and proceeded towards the end of the block. Ake's Tavern was on the ground floor of a three-storey plastoid building with wide, dark windows. An Imperial troop transport glided past Ezra, heading in the same direction. From what he could see, the transporter was carrying at least one squad of stormtroopers. Ezra had a bad feeling when he saw the transport, and decided that if it came to a stop in front of Ake's Tavern, he would keep walking.

The transport didn't stop. Ezra watched it travel another three blocks before it veered onto another street, and he lost sight of it. But the bad feeling didn't go away, not even after Ezra reminded himself that he was about to earn an easy thousand credits.

The door to Ake's Tavern was open. Ezra walked in. The tavern's interior was illuminated by dim orbs that drifted slowly through the air, just a few centimetres below the ceiling. A few customers sat on high seats around an L-shaped bar. The walls, tables, and seats were a strange mix of mismatched pieces scavenged from the cabins of decommissioned Republic cruisers.

A bald man with a thick beard stood behind the bar and was serving a drink to a lean Duros with bulbous, sleepy-looking eyes. The Duros sat beside a long-snouted Dug, who rested on his upper limbs. The Dug was using one of his dexterous feet to hold a drink while the toes of his other foot tapped at the bar's surface. To the left of the bar, a short distance from an arched doorway that Ezra guessed led to a back room, two Niktos, humanoids with scaled skin and facial horns, sat at an oval table that rested on three spindly legs. Both Niktos were seated so they faced the tavern's entrance, and they looked up as Ezra approached the bar.

The bartender, the Duros, and the Dug noticed Ezra walk in, too. Ezra didn't think anyone in the bar looked especially friendly. The bartender said, 'You look a bit young to be in here, kid.'

Ezra heard one Nikto mutter something to the other, but the only word he could make out was *backpack*.

His instincts told him to turn around and leave, but he thought again about the money he would earn from Bossk. He said, 'Is anyone here interested in tickets for the big fight tonight?'

The bartender narrowed his gaze on Ezra and said, 'You're selling tickets?'

'No, sir,' Ezra said. 'The fight's organisers authorised me to give away tickets. It's part of a promotion. You give me your name and contact information so the organizers can let you know about future promotions, and I'll give you a free ticket.'

The bartender said, 'What's the catch?'

'No catch, sir.' Ezra looked at the customers in the bar and said, 'If you'll all just give me your names, you'll each receive a ticket for –'

Ezra was interrupted by a loud scraping noise as one Nikto stood up and pushed his chair back across the floor. The Nikto carried two holstered blaster pistols, one on each hip. The Nikto faced the Duros and said in a deep voice, 'He matches the description of the kid with Bossk. Grab him.'

Ezra was surprised that the Nikto had been expecting him. With a blank expression, he looked from the Nikto to the Duros and said, 'Bossk? Who's Bossk?'

The second Nikto rose from his seat and held out a

sawed-off disruptor rifle. Ezra was considering whether he should make a run for the door or reach for his slingshot when he saw a shadowy figure appear in the arched doorway to the left of the bar. The figure stepped forwards, and Ezra saw it was Bossk.

Bossk held his mortar gun close to his body, with the barrel aimed straight in front of him. He opened fire, blasting the Nikto who held the disruptor rifle. As the Nikto fell, his finger clenched the rifle's trigger, causing the weapon to blast a wide hole in the ceiling just above the bar. Debris came crashing down. The second Nikto drew his blaster pistols and spun fast but Bossk fired again, and the second Nikto collapsed, knocking over the table beside him.

Ezra dropped to one knee and held his arm up protectively over his eyes while the bartender ducked down behind the bar. The Duros pushed himself away from the bar, fell back across the floor, and tugged his own blaster free from its holster as he rolled behind the table beside the dead Nikto. The Dug, using his upper limbs, jumped in the opposite direction over the bar and landed in a crouch, facing Ezra. One of the Dug's dexterous feet held a vibroblade, already activated and humming viciously.

Ezra knew that even the slightest contact with

a vibroblade could result in a lost limb or instant death. Faster than thought, he extended his left wrist. His slingshot snapped into place as his right hand flashed to his left and he pulled back on an energy ball. He released the ball and it smashed into the Dug's forehead. The stunned Dug fell back, hitting the back of his head against the base of the bar as his vibroblade skittered away from him and carved a long, deep gouge in the floor before it shut off automatically. The Dug lay motionless.

Debris continued to rain down from the blasted hole in the ceiling, blocking Ezra's view of Bossk's position at the back of the tavern. Still down on one knee with his slingshot aimed at the unconscious Dug, Ezra looked to the Duros, who remained crouched behind the fallen table. The Duros had his blaster aimed at Ezra. Ezra froze.

The Duros said, 'Drop your weapon, Bossk, or I'll shoot the boy.'

Ezra could not see Bossk through the cloud of dust and smoke that now filled the tavern, but he heard him make a hacking sound and realised the Trandoshan was laughing. But then the laughter stopped abruptly, and Bossk said, 'You really think the kid's worth anything to me?' Before the Duros could reply, Bossk added, 'Hey, shorty. Is the Dug still breathing?'

Ezra glanced at the Dug and said, 'Yes.' The word was barely out of his mouth when Bossk's mortar gun fired again. Ezra closed his eyes reflexively, and when he opened them, all that remained of the fallen table was one twisted leg. He couldn't see much left of the Duros either.

The tavern's air was thick with the smell of blaster fire as well as a haze of dust. Ezra saw Bossk emerge from the haze and step over the remains of the table. From behind the bar, the bartender said, 'Is it over?'

'Shut up, barkeep,' Bossk snapped, 'and stay down.'

Ezra stood up slowly. 'This is a lot more than I bargained for, Mr Bossk. If you won't be needing me anymore, I'll just take the money you owe me and be on my way.'

Bossk snorted, sending a spray of dust from his broad nostrils. 'In case you didn't notice, I'm a little busy at the moment.'

'But –'

Bossk crouched beside the unconscious Dug and said, 'Hello, Shifty. Can you hear me? Wake up!' He slapped the Dug hard across the face.

The Dug moaned and opened his eyes. Bossk said, 'Gronson Takkaro, by the authority of the Bounty Hunters Guild, you are now my acquisition.' He tapped a sharp-clawed finger against the Dug's forehead, causing the Dug to wince. 'How'd a casino clown like you wind up with professional assassins like Angrigo and the Kratchell twins?'

Shifty cleared his throat. 'The Duros . . . and the two Niktos? I didn't even know their names! They just got here a few minutes ago . . . said they came to protect me.'

'From who?'

'A bounty hunter. You!'

Bossk snarled. 'Who hired them?'

Shifty shook his long-snouted head against the floor. 'I don't know. Ask them.'

Bossk laughed, and his hacking noise was louder than before. 'That's funny, Shifty. I *would* ask them, but you see, Angrigo and both Kratchells are kinda dead.'

Shifty's eyes rolled back in their sockets and he passed out. Bossk was about to slap him again when he and Ezra heard repulsorlift engines slow to a stop outside the tavern. They saw shadows flicker through the haze, then heard familiar clanking noises that they recognised as stormtroopers in motion. Ezra said, 'Sounds like we have trouble, Mr Bossk.'

From outside, as if in response, an amplified voice boomed, 'IMPERIAL AUTHORITIES HAVE YOU SURROUNDED! PUT DOWN YOUR WEAPONS!'

Bossk snorted again. 'Idiots,' he muttered as he rose and walked towards the entrance, stopping short of the door. Still holding his mortar gun, he shouted, 'Listen up, out there! My name's Bossk, and I'm a licensed bounty hunter. My Imperial Peace-Keeping Certificate number is five-five-nine-four-six-one-one-two. I have four acquisitions in here. Three assassins and a bail jumper. My hunt for the bail jumper and my presence on Lothal was sanctioned by Lieutenant Herdringer of the Imperial Security Bureau. Contact Herdringer, and he'll verify that.'

Ezra held his breath as he listened for the stormtrooper's response. The dust in the tavern was beginning to settle, and he could almost see the doorway at the back of the room. He wondered if stormtroopers would try to enter the building from the rear, or if that route would offer an opportunity for escape. He was still considering the best way to avoid the Imperials when the stormtrooper outside responded, 'YOUR ASSIGNMENT WAS NOT SANCTIONED. PUT DOWN YOUR WEAPONS AND STEP OUTSIDE IMMEDIATELY!'

From behind the bar, the hidden bartender whimpered, 'I think it would be best to surrender.'

'Shut up,' Bossk snapped.

Ezra looked at Bossk and saw the Trandoshan's scaled brow furrow. Bossk muttered, 'The rat set me up.'

Confused, Ezra said, 'Who?'

'The Imperial officer who told me where to find Shifty.' Bossk reached to the back of his belt and removed a concussion grenade. He grabbed Shifty and flung the Dug's limp body over his shoulder. He pushed the grenade's trigger, tossed the grenade out through the open doorway, and then ran towards the back of the tavern, taking Shifty with him, while Ezra took cover beside the bar.

The explosion made the tavern's windows buckle in their frames and sent a stormtrooper's helmet bouncing in through the front door. The helmet tumbled across the floor and skidded to a stop near Ezra. Ezra grabbed it. His ears were still ringing from the explosion, but he heard muffled shouts from outside. The grenade's blast had also kicked up more dust in the tavern, causing him to lose sight of Bossk.

Ezra knew that stormtrooper helmets were equipped with advanced optical sensors. He placed the helmet over his head and scanned the room. Through the helmet's lenses, he saw thermal readouts for two stormtroopers as they rushed in through the back doorway. He also saw Bossk, who had positioned himself and the unconscious Shifty behind a fallen table.

As Bossk reloaded his mortar gun with stun cartridges, the stormtroopers opened fire. Bossk returned fire as he jumped away from Shifty and rolled across the debris-littered floor. The stunning blasts knocked both troopers off their feet, and their armour clattered as they fell.

Still wearing the stormtrooper helmet, Ezra yelled, 'Mr Bossk! Don't shoot me!' He ran past Bossk, bent down beside one of the fallen stormtroopers, and snatched up the trooper's blaster rifle.

Looking down at Ezra, Bossk chortled. 'Aren't you a little short for a stormtrooper?'

Ezra ignored the comment and said, 'We have to get out of here!'

'No kidding. Give me a hand with Shifty.'

'Forget the Dug!' Ezra said.

'I'm not leaving without him. He's too valuable.'

'Well, I'm leaving now!' Ezra tilted his helmeted head back to look up at the Nikto-blasted hole in the ceiling. With the stormtrooper's blaster rifle in one hand, he ran towards the bar, jumped up onto a stool, and then onto the bar itself. He crouched and sprang up through the hole.

Ezra cleared the edges of the hole and rolled onto the floor above the bar. He stood up and looked around to see he was in a storage room. The Nikto's blast had struck several crates of dried food, and also scattered several crates away from the blast radius. Ezra saw a door on the far side of the room.

Moving away from the hole in the floor, he heard a loud thud behind him and glanced back to see Bossk had jumped up after him. Bossk clutched his mortar gun with one hand, and carried Shifty with the other.

Ezra said, 'There's a door this way.'

'The troopers will have that covered,' Bossk said. 'Gotta find another way out.' Holding his mortar gun in front of him, he draped Shifty over one shoulder, kicked aside a crate in his path, and led Ezra towards a wide, transparent plastic window. The window overlooked the street in front of the tavern's entrance. Two troop transports were parked at angles in the street, blocking traffic. Several stormtroopers had assumed defensive positions around the vehicles and were directing pedestrians to leave the area. Ezra followed Bossk's gaze. He counted five unconscious stormtroopers, including the one who had lost his helmet to Ezra.

Two Imperial scout troopers on speeder bikes came to a stop beside one transporter. Like the stormtroopers, the scouts wore white helmets and armour, but their helmets had more sophisticated sensors. Their armour was also lighter in weight and designed to allow them to climb on and off their bikes rapidly.

Thinking fast, Ezra activated his helmet's built-in comlink. He lowered his voice and said, 'The bounty hunter is heading for the roof. We have him in our sights.' He deactivated the comlink.

Bossk said, 'Nice work, shorty.' He plucked the blaster rifle from Ezra's hands and aimed in the general direction of the second floor's back door. He squeezed off several shots, launching red laserfire across the storage room. He looked out the window and saw the stormtroopers and one scout trooper running away from their defensive positions and heading around to the side of the tavern. Only one scout trooper remained with the vehicles. The two speeder bikes hovered motionlessly beside him.

Bossk aimed the rifle at the window and fired. The window shattered. He used the rifle's butt to knock out the remaining plastic shards from the window's frame, then he shoved the rifle back at Ezra, who took it. Bossk said, 'You want to earn more money? Stick with me.'

Still carrying Shifty, Bossk leapt out through the open window, landing on top of the troop transport. The lone scout trooper heard Bossk's impact and turned in response. Bossk pounced. As he landed on the scout and rammed him into the street's hard surface, Shifty fell away from Bossk's back.

Clutching the blaster rifle, Ezra followed Bossk out the window. He landed on the transport and jumped down to the street. Through his helmet's enhanced optics, he sighted an Imperial surveillance remote hovering a short distance from the transport. The remote began to rise but Ezra raised his blaster rifle and destroyed it with a single shot.

Bossk lifted Shifty up from the ground and placed him on the back of a speeder bike before he climbed into the bike's saddle. Ezra moved towards the other bike but stopped short when he heard a stormtrooper call out, 'Look! Over there! Stop him!'

A hail of laserfire streaked past Ezra and struck Shifty's body so hard that the Dug was knocked off the back of the speeder bike. Bossk cursed as he let Shifty fall. The stormtroopers fired again, and Ezra leapt and landed on the back of Bossk's saddle. Ezra gripped the back of Bossk's belt with his free hand while he clung to the blaster rifle with the other. Bossk punched the ignition and they zoomed off up the street.

The speed was incredible, and Ezra tightened his grip on Bossk's belt. He turned his helmeted head to glance back at the tavern and troop transports, but the speeder bike had already travelled so far that he could barely see their departure point in the distance.

Bossk guided the bike to the middle of the street so they travelled between two lanes of traffic. He shouted, 'Anyone following us?'

Ezra said, 'I don't think they . . . Wait! I see a scout!'

The scout trooper was crouched down low over his bike's controls. He fired the bike's cannons at Bossk's bike, but Bossk veered to the side, and the laserfire sailed past him. Bossk shouted, 'Don't just sit there, shorty. You have a blaster rifle. Use it!'

Ezra extended the blaster rifle and tried to return fire, but the rifle only produced a loud clicking noise. 'It's jammed! You must have busted it when you used it to clear the glass from the window.' Ezra threw the blaster rifle at the scout trooper, but the scout saw it whipping through the air at him, and he banked sideways. The rifle bounced off the bottom of the scout's bike and fell to the road.

Bossk snarled as he headed for a multilevel highway intersection. Because he was moving so fast, other traffic appeared to be moving at a ridiculously sluggish speed.

The scout trooper fired again, and a laser bolt glanced off Ezra's helmet. Bossk shifted one hand's grip on the manoeuvring controls as he yanked his mortar gun free with the other. He swung the gun back and fired at the scout trooper. All the shots went wild. Bossk said, 'Can you handle this bike?'

'I think so, but –'

'Good enough,' Bossk said. With one fluid motion, he removed his hand from the bike's controls, reached behind himself to grab Ezra, and then moved himself to the back of the bike while quickly depositing Ezra directly in front of him.

Ezra grabbed the Imperial speeder bike's controls. He had some experience with riding jump speeders and found the speeder bike's controls weren't much different.

Bossk twisted his upper body and raised his mortar gun to fire at the scout trooper, but Ezra wasn't prepared for the way Bossk shifted his weight, and their own speeder bike dipped to the right. The stormtrooper helmet nearly slid off Ezra's head.

The scout trooper fired an energy bolt that whizzed past Bossk's head. Bossk cursed as Ezra wrestled with the controls. Ezra levelled off and Bossk raised his mortar gun again. Bossk fired, and the blast caught the scout square against his armoured chest plate. The scout fell away from his bike and tumbled onto the street. His bike spiralled and smashed into a pylon below a highway overpass.

Ezra detected two needle-like shadows that travelled on the road just ahead of him. He looked up to see two additional scout troopers on speeder bikes following his trajectory and bearing down on his position. He said, 'We've got more company, Mr Bossk.'

The scout troopers drew their blaster pistols and fired down at Ezra and Bossk. Bossk fired back at them, but they took evasive action, weaving to avoid his blasts. They fired again, and one laserbolt pinged off the back of the bike near Bossk's left leg. Bossk said, 'We need to take cover!'

'There's a fork up ahead that leads into the east cross-town tunnel,' Ezra said. 'We can lose them in there.'

The scout troopers fired again. Bossk said, 'Better get us into that tunnel soon, kid!'

Ezra raced around a sanitation repulsortruck and a

droid-operated taxi, and then saw the approaching fork. From above, the scout troopers fired again, sending laserfire into the road in front of Ezra, momentarily distracting him. He thought he'd missed the fork, but then sighted a curving ramp and went for it.

The speeder bike plunged into the mouth of an oval-shaped tunnel. Both Ezra and Bossk immediately saw a series of oncoming landspeeders and realised they were on a collision course. Ezra yelled, 'I entered the wrong tunnel!'

'Fry me,' said Bossk.

# CHAPTER 4
# A NARROW ESCAPE

**Ezra moved fast,** swinging the speeder bike close to the tunnel's ceiling to avoid hitting a wide repulsortruck. He had to simultaneously accelerate and descend to steer clear of a late-model landspeeder's flared spoilers. Although the tunnel was wide enough for a speeder bike pilot to make a full turn, the oncoming vehicles were approaching so fast that all Ezra could do was focus on what was immediately in front of him.

In an open-air landspeeder, a tall Anx with a crested head shrieked and ducked as Ezra sped over his vehicle. Through the lenses of his stormtrooper helmet, Ezra caught fleeting glimpses of people inside their landspeeders, and most of them wore panicked expressions as they sighted him and Bossk. Ezra imagined that the sight of a fourteen-year-old boy wearing a stormtrooper helmet while riding a speeder bike with a Trandoshan would probably surprise him too.

Behind Ezra, Bossk cursed again. Ezra considered suggesting that they leap from the speeder bike and try to land on a vehicle travelling in the opposite direction, but as a series of drivers hit their horns and flashed their lights, he suspected he and Bossk might live longer if they remained airborne.

Over the roar of traffic and howling engines, Ezra said, 'Look on the bright side, Mr Bossk. Those scout troopers won't dare follow us in here.'

Bright bursts of red laserfire erupted from behind and zinged past Ezra and Bossk. Bossk leant forwards, placing his jaws close beside Ezra's helmet, and said, 'Oh, they won't, won't they?'

Ezra tapped the accelerator. Bossk turned at the waist, sighted the two scout troopers who had pursued them into the tunnel, and fired his gun. In trying to avoid the blast, one scout trooper veered into the tunnel's wall and bounced off it. The scout trooper and his bike crashed to the tunnel's floor, prompting several oncoming repulsorlift vehicles to swerve around him. Three vehicles collided, and the tunnel was suddenly filled with the noise of airspeeders activating their emergency braking flaps.

The remaining scout trooper ignored his fallen comrade and continued his pursuit of Ezra and Bossk. He manoeuvred behind them and fired his laser cannons. Ezra weaved erratically in a desperate attempt to avoid a direct hit while Bossk returned fire at the scout.

A laserbolt tore through Bossk's upper shoulder. The Trandoshan let out a low grunt but barely flinched. He instinctively calculated the scout trooper's trajectory and aimed his weapon a short distance in front of the bike. Bossk fired. The scout's directional steering vanes caught the full blast, and his bike fell like a stone. The scout clung to the controls as the bike hit the road and skidded between two lanes of oncoming traffic.

'Gotcha!' Bossk said. He tapped the side of Ezra's helmet and said, 'Use the built-in data display to find data to get us out of here.'

Keeping his eyes forwards, Ezra saw illuminated numbers and perspective grids appear through his helmet's optical sensors. He said, 'There's a fork in the tunnel, about half a kilometre away. It looks like the left fork will get us out of the tunnel faster.'

'Then take it.'

Ezra thought Bossk's voice sounded strained.

Seconds later, with traffic still flowing in the opposite direction beneath him, Ezra swung into the left fork. The branch of the tunnel curved sharply, and Bossk leant hard to his left to prevent the bike from overturning. The curved stretch delivered them into a long straight, and Ezra saw the mouth of the tunnel in the distance. He tapped the accelerator and raced over more oncoming vehicles as he headed for the tunnel's mouth.

The speeder bike launched out of the tunnel and over a stream of traffic. Ezra took a sharp right turn into a side street that was lined with low buildings. Beyond the buildings, Ezra saw grassy plains and realised they'd reached the edge of the city.

Bossk pointed to a shadowy gap between two buildings and said, 'That alley. Get us there.'

Ezra manoeuvred the speeder bike into the alley. The bike's thrusters sputtered as it came to a hovering stop near one building's ventilation units. Bossk shoved himself off the bike. Staying in the shadows, he ran back to the opening of the alley and looked around. A siren sounded in the distance. When the siren faded, Bossk walked back towards Ezra and said, 'No one followed us.'

Ezra pulled off his helmet. 'Mr Bossk, you said that

if I stuck with you, I'd earn more money. You already owe me a thousand for going into Ake's Tavern.'

'No, I don't,' Bossk said as he leant against a ventilation unit. 'You didn't do as I said.'

*'What?'*

'I told you to go in and say, "Is someone here waiting for Mr Bossk?" and then say, "Mr Bossk will be here in a moment." But that's not what you did. You went in talking nonsense, offering to sell tickets to a big fight. You made those assassins jumpy.'

'Jumpy? That's ridiculous! One look at those guys, and my gut told me they were all trigger-happy. I knew if I mentioned your name, they'd blast me.'

Bossk made a hacking noise. Ezra thought the Trandoshan was laughing. Ezra said, 'Hang on. You said you forgot the name of the guy you were supposed to meet, and that you'd wait for me outside the tavern. But you sneaked in through the back door, and you knew the name of that Shifty guy, and also the names of the Duros and the Niktos.' Ezra moved closer to Bossk. 'You used me as a decoy!'

Bossk hacked again, and it was only then that Ezra noticed Bossk's shoulder was covered with blood. Ezra realised Bossk wasn't laughing. He was gasping.

'Listen carefully, shorty,' Bossk said. 'An Imperial

Security Bureau officer, Lieutenant Herdringer . . . I talked with him by holocomm before I landed on Lothal. Herdringer told me that I'd find Shifty at the tavern. I believe he also set me up to die. I can't go back to my ship because stormtroopers will be watching for me, and I . . . I'm wounded. I need a place to recover. A safe place. I'll figure out a way back to my ship later. Just . . . get me out of here.'

'Why should I?' Ezra said. 'You used me as a decoy, and you chiselled me out of a thousand credits!'

Bossk let out a harsh wheeze. 'On my ship, there's a strongbox. You can have all the money in it . . . if you just help me . . .'

Bossk fell away from the ventilation unit and collapsed on the alley floor.

Inside his office that overlooked the Lothal spaceport, Lieutenant Jenkes was in the process of erasing data from his computer when his holocomm console chirped. He turned to face the console and a hologram of the stormtrooper TK-5331 appeared. 'TK-5331 at checkpoint five to Lieutenant Jenkes.'

Jenkes said, 'Yes?'

'Squad Five reports three dead at Ake's Tavern. The bodies have been identified as assassins, all with bounties on their heads. A Dug criminal was injured. Squad Five apprehended him.'

'What about the bounty hunter?'

'He fled, sir.'

Jenkes struggled to remain calm. 'Fled?'

'He and his associate stole a speeder bike and escaped in a landspeeder expressway tunnel. Three scouts were wounded while pursuing them.'

'His associate?'

'A young male, sir. We believe he's the same boy who accompanied the hunter from the spaceport.'

'What about Squad Five's remotes? Did they identify the boy?'

'No, sir,' said TK-5331. 'A single remote sighted the suspect, but the suspect blasted it. The remote's final transmission showed the suspect wearing a helmet that he stole from our troops.'

'In other words, you've no idea who the boy is, or where he went with the hunter.'

'Affirmative, sir,' the stormtrooper said sheepishly. 'But they can't get far. We have sentries posted around the hunter's ship as well as throughout the spaceport. Also, one of our scouts reported that he's certain the hunter took a direct hit during the chase through the tunnel.'

'Can the scout confirm the hunter was killed?'

'No, sir.'

'Then notify all troops to watch for the hunter and his young accomplice,' Jenkes said. 'For crimes against the Empire, they must be exterminated.'

'Yes, sir.'

# CHAPTER 5
# MASTER OF DISGUISE

**Bossk groaned.** He opened his eyes and realised he was no longer in the alley between the two buildings at the edge of the city. He was lying on a mat that was stretched across three dusty storage crates in a room that was cluttered with old, rusted machinery. A wide, thick bandage was wrapped around his wounded shoulder. He shifted his eyes and found Ezra seated on a grime-stained metal bench. He had his newly acquired stormtrooper helmet on his lap and was using a small tool to remove its comlink component.

Bossk said, 'Where am I?' He sniffed at the air. 'We're not in the city anymore.'

Ezra set the helmet aside. 'I brought you to an abandoned communications tower, outside the city limits. No one will look for us here.'

'Where's my gun?'

'Right there,' Ezra said as he gestured to the wall beside the room's only door. Bossk's mortar gun leant against the edge of the doorway beside Ezra's backpack. Ezra had already emptied the backpack of recently stolen valuables.

Bossk sniffed the air again. 'This is your home.'

'No, it isn't,' Ezra lied. 'I just stay here sometimes.'

Bossk blinked. 'How long was I out?'

'About an hour.' Ezra picked up the helmet and pried out the comlink. He placed it in his jacket pocket and put the helmet down on the bench.

Bossk sat up slowly and examined his bandaged shoulder. 'Looks like you used two Imperial medpacs on me.'

Ezra nodded. 'The medpacs were in the speeder bike's cargo compartment. After I stopped the bleeding, I hauled you onto the speeder bike and strapped you down behind me. Except for waiting for an Imperial patrol to pass, I didn't have any trouble getting here. I made sure I wasn't followed.'

Bossk snorted. 'Glad to know you did something right.'

'What's that supposed to mean?'

'You took us into the wrong tunnel!'

'Yeah, but then I helped you, didn't I? I bandaged

you, and I got you out of that alley. And I may as well tell you, putting you on the bike wasn't easy. You're heavy.'

'I didn't ask for your help, weakling,' Bossk said. 'If you'd just left me in that alley to bleed to death, I wouldn't have to listen to you complain.'

Ezra scowled. 'But you did ask for my help! You said if I got you to a safe place to recover, you'd give me all the money in your ship's strongbox. Remember?'

Bossk's eyes widened. 'I told you about my strongbox?'

'How else would I know about it?'

Bossk swallowed hard. 'I said *all* the money?'

'Yes. All of it.'

'But . . . I must have been delirious!'

'Mr Bossk, it's my understanding that you're a professional businessman. I expect you to honour that deal.'

Bossk snarled, took a deep breath, and then let out a long sigh. 'All right, shorty. You got me. All the money in the strongbox is yours.'

'Just how much money are we talking about?'

'Maybe more than you can lift. And if I could give it to you right now, I would. The trouble is the spaceport is probably crawling with stormtroopers by now, and they'll all have their sights set on me.'

Ezra said, 'You think they'll board your ship?'

'Don't worry about your money. I already mentioned my ship's security system. If any stormtroopers get too close to it, they'll be vaporised.' Bossk swung his thick legs over the edge of the mat and planted his bare feet on the floor.

Ezra said, 'You should probably rest some more. You lost a lot of blood.'

'I'm more concerned about losing time,' Bossk said as he stood up. 'What happened back at Ake's Tavern was no accident. Lieutenant Herdringer set me up. I want to know why he set me up, and I want to set things straight. I'm not leaving Lothal until I get paid for taking down three assassins at Ake's Tavern, and I'm compensated for the loss of Shifty.'

Ezra raised his eyebrows. 'What else do you want? An apology from Herdringer?'

'No,' Bossk said. 'I want an apology from his superiors.'

Ezra wondered if Bossk were indeed delirious. He said, 'I suppose you also expect Herdringer will get arrested?'

'No,' Bossk said, and the edges of his mouth twisted into a wicked smile. 'I expect he'll get worse.' Bossk walked towards the door. 'I gotta get some fresh air.'

Ezra had rigged his tower with numerous traps and devices to discourage trespassers, so he moved fast in front of Bossk and said, 'Careful. I noticed some stuff with sharp edges lying around.' He grabbed his backpack and shrugged it on before he went through the doorway.

Bossk picked up his mortar gun and followed Ezra into a cluttered corridor, then through another doorway that led outside. Across the plains, the larger buildings and cooling towers of Capital City loomed on the horizon. Bossk turned and scanned the base of the communications tower. 'Where's the speeder bike?'

'I hid it around back. It got pretty beaten up.'

'It's no use to us anyway,' Bossk said. 'Imperials will be on the lookout for a stolen bike. We got any other transportation around here?'

Ezra nodded. 'There's an old jump bike in the garage.'

'Get it. We're leaving.'

'Where?'

'Back to the spaceport. I need to get to a posting agency with access to the Imperial Enforcement DataCore. I aim to find out how those assassins wound up on Lothal.'

Ezra said, 'Posting agency?'

Bossk snorted. 'Where bounties get posted!

We passed one in the concourse when we left the spaceport.'

'But won't stormtroopers be stationed there?'

'Maybe. If we see any, I'll deal with them.'

'Mr Bossk, we already had a nasty run-in with troopers today. I don't think you're in shape for another round.'

'It'll be a breeze. And if you want all the money in my strongbox, this time you'll do exactly what I say. Now get the jump bike.'

'Well . . . all right.' Ezra went into the garage. The hovering jump bike was covered by a dusty tarpaulin that had once been a dark green but had faded over time. Leaving the tarp on, Ezra pushed the bike through the air, bringing it outside. Bossk walked over to the bike and lifted the tarp away. The old bike consisted of an inexpensive repulsorlift engine, basic manoeuvre controls, and a pair of small thrusters. A set of dark goggles dangled from the manoeuvre controls. The bike's surface was pocked with numerous dents.

'What a piece of junk,' Bossk said. 'You sure it will carry both of us?'

'It's sturdier than it looks,' Ezra said. 'Too bad it leaves us exposed. Anyone looking for a Trandoshan is bound to see you.'

'Good thing I'm a master of disguise,' Bossk said. He reached for the goggles that dangled from the bike. He wrapped the strap of the goggles around the back of his head and lowered the dark lenses over his eyes. Then he took the dusty tarp and quickly tied it around the collar of his flight suit, transforming it into a cape that draped around his shoulders and covered most of his upper body. 'How do I look?'

'Like a Trandoshan bounty hunter wearing goggles and a dirty blanket.'

'Ah,' Bossk said. 'But how do I look when I do *this*?' He held his sharp-clawed hands out in front of him and tilted his head so that he appeared to be looking at something behind Ezra. He moved his hands back and forth as he took a slight step forwards and bumped into the side of the floating jump bike.

Ezra said, 'Like a *clumsy* Trandoshan bounty hunter wearing goggles and a dirty blanket?'

'No, you idiot,' Bossk said. 'I look like a blind tourist.'

'Oh,' Ezra said, because he didn't know what else to say. 'That's very, um . . .'

'Clever, huh?'

'Not exactly the word I was thinking.'

'No one will ever recognise me.' Bossk tucked his mortar gun under one arm, then swung a leg over the jump bike's saddle and sat down behind the controls. He patted the back of the saddle and said, 'Climb on.'

Ezra remained standing beside the bike. 'If the goal of your disguise is to convince people that you're unable to see anything, don't you think it would be more practical if *I* handled the bike?'

Bossk muttered a curse as he slid back on the seat until he straddled the bike's repulsorlift engine. Ezra climbed onto the saddle in front of Bossk, gunned the bike's engine, and they took off, racing away from the communications tower.


Lieutenant Jenkes was seated in his office when his door slid open and a droid walked in. It was a black-metal RA-7 protocol droid with an insectoid head. Jenkes said, 'Any update on the bounty hunter?'

'No, Lieutenant,' the RA-7 replied.

Jenkes scowled. 'Then what do you have to report?'

'Item one. Squad Seven arrested two miners who attempted to escape a labour camp. Item two. Your appointment with Commandant Aresko has been rescheduled for tomorrow. Item three. A surveillance droid has observed unusual activity in the vicinity of Monad Outpost. Item four. The local spaceport authority reports a –'

'Hold on,' Jenkes interrupted. 'Back to Monad Outpost. What did the surveillance droid see?'

The RA-7 made a clicking noise as it accessed data, then said, 'Numerous civilians have begun congregating near the decommissioned docking bays.'

Jenkes pursed his lips. 'The surveillance droid has witnessed a highly classified Imperial project. Instruct the droid to return to the city at once, and have its memory wiped.'

'Yes, Lieutenant.' The RA-7 made more clicking noises as its metal head tilted towards the office's communications console.

Jenkes said, 'What was the rest of item four?'

'Item four. The local spaceport authority reports a freighter from Nyriaan has requested permission to land. The freighter's manifest indicates it is transporting livestock, but sensors indicate –'

'Inform the spaceport authority that the freighter has permission to land by my authorisation,' Jenkes said.

'Yes, Lieutenant,' said the RA-7. 'Do you have any orders?'

Jenkes thought for a moment, then said, 'If anyone examines my data on the Imperial Enforcement DataCore, you'll notify me immediately.'

'Yes, Lieutenant.'

'You are dismissed.'

The RA-7 exited his office. Jenkes walked to his window that overlooked the spaceport. He saw the freighter from Nyriaan as it descended to a landing pad. 'Right on time,' he said.

Jenkes picked up his macrobinoculars and continued to watch the freighter as it touched down. An unmarked Imperial transport moved across the spaceport and came to a stop beside the freighter. The freighter's wide hatch opened and two large aliens lumbered down the boarding ramp. One alien was a bare-chested Houk with massive forearms. The other was a tall Feeorin who wore body armour and had thick tendrils hanging from the back of his head. The two aliens ducked into the unmarked transport, and then the transport sped away from the shuttle, heading for a route out of the city.

Jenkes made a mental note to either have the RA-7's memory erased or destroy it himself.

# CHAPTER 6
# THE POSTING AGENCY

**'Can't this** contraption go any faster?' Bossk said as he shifted his haunches on the jump bike's thrusters.

'Stop wiggling,' Ezra said, 'or you'll throw us off balance!'

The faded green tarp whipped at Bossk's back as the jump bike carried him and Ezra over the grassy plains of Lothal. They reached a hilly area, and Ezra wove through and around the hills, moving closer to the city while keeping his eyes peeled for Imperial patrols.

They passed a cluster of ramshackle farm buildings before they approached a road used primarily by industrial repulsorlift vehicles. Ezra swung the bike over the road and slid into traffic between an ore-hauler and a convoy of Imperial supplies transports.

Bossk said, 'This isn't the way to the spaceport.'

'I'm taking an indirect route,' Ezra said. 'By going this way, we'll avoid the Imperial checkpoints.'

Ezra stuck close to the back of one transport and followed it until he saw a row of power stations at the edge of the city. Bossk dug his claws into the sides of the bike's thrusters as Ezra made a sharp turn onto a service road, which led them past the power stations.

Bossk said, 'If you're so concerned about checkpoints, you should have worn a disguise too.'

'Stop wiggling!' Ezra said. 'Please!' He steered away from the power stations and onto another service road that curved around a complex of warehouses and modular box-shaped outbuildings. He veered into an alley between two buildings without windows and brought the bike to a stop beside two bulkheads near the end of the alley.

Ezra climbed off the jump bike. 'We'll leave the bike here and walk the rest of the way to the spaceport. It's not far.'

Bossk eased himself off the bike and adjusted the tarp around his body to make sure his makeshift cape covered his mortar gun. Ezra pushed the bike between the bulkheads, tucking it in to prevent others from seeing it. He turned to face Bossk, who was brushing dust off the lenses of his goggles. Ezra said,

'If you're pretending to be blind, shouldn't you have a walking stick?'

'I got something better,' Bossk said. He planted one of his claws on Ezra's shoulder. 'You'll be my seeing-eye boy.'

Ezra stared at Bossk with astonishment. 'You've got to be kidding me.'

'You want all the money in my strongbox, or don't you? Start walking.'

With Bossk holding his shoulder and trailing at his heels, Ezra began walking out of the alley. They were already so close to the spaceport that they could hear the rumble of space freighter engines.

Ezra led Bossk into a courtyard that was shared by workers from a landspeeder maintenance garage and a droid service center. Outside the garage's open bay, a group of mechanics wearing oil-stained overalls was seated at a metal table, taking a lunch break. Bossk ignored the mechanics and kept his goggled gaze focused directly in front of him.

Ezra glanced at the mechanics and noticed a few were gazing at him and Bossk. Distracted, he didn't notice an electric cable that snaked across the courtyard's floor from the droid service center. He stumbled over it, but Bossk rapidly shifted his grip to catch Ezra's backpack, which stopped Ezra from falling.

One mechanic, a lean man with blond hair, called out, 'You two OK?'

'We're fine,' Ezra said as he moved past the cable. 'Just taking a shortcut to the spaceport.'

Bossk returned his grip to Ezra's shoulder and gave Ezra a slight shove. Bossk said loudly, 'Move faster, boy! My shuttle leaves in five minutes.'

'Yes, sir,' Ezra said. He began walking faster. He stole another glance at the mechanics and saw that they'd returned their attention to their meals.

When Ezra and Bossk were beyond the mechanics' earshot, Bossk said, 'In case you're wondering, I said I was leaving on a shuttle to make those guys lose interest in us. To them, I'm just a tourist who's on his way off this rock.'

'I sure hope that's all they thought,' Ezra said. 'Because if any Imperials ask them if they saw a Trandoshan, they may –'

'My disguise is foolproof! So stop worrying about people looking at us, and just keep moving.'

Ezra led Bossk through another alley and they emerged on a crowded market street at the edge of the spaceport's main concourse. Ezra noticed that Bossk, even while disguised as a blind Trandoshan, seemed to naturally discourage other life-forms from getting too close.

Bossk's eyes shifted behind his dark goggles as he scanned the buildings on the street. The buildings were modular structures that ranged in height from three to five storeys. Bossk said, 'The posting agency is five buildings to the left, the one with the holosigns over the entrance.'

'I see it,' Ezra said. The holosigns displayed three-dimensional views of wanted criminals. As he pretended to guide Bossk through the crowd, he spied four stormtroopers across the street from the posting agency. The stormtroopers were standing on a stairway, two steps above street level, that led into an Imperial substation, and gave them a clear view of everyone on the street. Two stormtroopers were facing each other and appeared to be talking while the other two monitored pedestrian traffic. All four held blaster rifles.

Bossk patted Ezra's shoulder. 'I see the white-bucket squad, too. You distract them while I go into the posting office.'

'It's too late for a distraction,' Ezra said. 'One of the troopers is looking right at us. But I know how to deal with him.' Ezra began walking straight for the stormtroopers.

Bossk kept his grip on Ezra's shoulder and shuffled along behind him. 'Don't make any stupid moves, kid.'

Ezra led Bossk over to the stormtroopers and came to a stop at the bottom of the stairway. Bossk kept his head lowered so that he appeared to be staring at the back of Ezra's neck. The two stormtroopers who were talking to each other continued their conversation while one of the two other troopers looked down at Ezra.

'Excuse me, sir,' Ezra said. 'Could you please direct me to the nearest posting agency?'

'Over there,' the stormtrooper replied. He shifted his armoured arms slightly to make the tip of his blaster rifle point at the building across the street.

'Thank you, sir.'

Ezra had begun to lead Bossk away from the bottom of the stairway when the stormtrooper said, 'Stop there.'

Ezra stopped fast, causing Bossk to bump into him. Ezra turned to look back at the stormtrooper and said, 'Yes, sir?'

The stormtrooper tilted his head so the chin of his helmet jutted towards Bossk. 'Why's he holding you like that?'

Ezra nodded. 'He's blind, sir.'

'Oh,' said the stormtrooper. He looked away, turning his helmet to survey a group of passing pedestrians.

Ezra resumed walking. As he led Bossk into the posting office, he said, 'OK, I admit it. I was wrong about your disguise. It sure fooled that trooper.'

'That's because fools believe what they see,' Bossk said. 'If they see someone who looks harmless, they don't feel threatened.'

Inside the posting agency, several computer consoles were lined up along one wall. Above the consoles, holographic data displays of criminals flickered just below the ceiling. Bossk also noticed a single ceiling-mounted security holocam.

One computer console was being used by a rangy-looking Ranat, a metre-tall rodent-like alien with long incisors that protruded from his lower jaw. The Ranat's long tail twitched back and forth as he reviewed data on his console's monitor. Another console was occupied by a broad-shouldered Nimbanel who wore a large space helmet. The helmet's dark visor was raised, revealing the Nimbanel's small black eyes and heavy jowls. Both the Ranat and the Nimbanel carried holstered blasters, and Ezra assumed they were bounty hunters.

At the far end of the room was a booth with a

blaster-proof transparisteel window. Behind the window, a Sakiyan with a bulbous skull and sharply tapered ears sat on a chair before a control console and switchboard. The Sakiyan glanced at Ezra and Bossk before he returned his attention to his screen.

Bossk's eyes shifted back and forth behind his goggles as he examined the office's layout, but he kept his head still as he said, 'Tell me, boy, can you see the posting agent? Is he available?'

Ezra realised Bossk was talking about the Sakiyan. Ezra said, 'There's a man seated inside a booth, sir.'

'Bring me to him.'

Ezra led Bossk around the Ranat, who drew his tail close to his feet to prevent the Trandoshan from stepping on it, and brought Bossk to a stop in front of the Sakiyan's booth. On the other side of the window, the Sakiyan looked up at Bossk. Seeing that the goggled Trandoshan seemed to be staring at his young companion's head, the Sakiyan shifted his gaze to Ezra and said, 'Want something?'

Bossk said, 'That the agent talking?'

'I think so, sir,' Ezra said. Facing the Sakiyan, he said, 'Sir, you are the posting agent, yes?'

The Sakiyan looked back to Bossk and cleared his

throat. 'Yes. I am. How may I be of service?'

Bossk said, 'Does this office have links for the Imperial Enforcement DataCore?'

'Yes,' the Sakiyan said. 'But access is limited to Imperial personnel and licensed bounty hunters.'

'I got a licence,' Bossk said. Pushing his cape back without revealing his mortar gun, he reached into a pocket and pulled out a plastic card. He held the card out in front of him. Ezra took the card and held it up to the window so the Sakiyan could see it.

The Sakiyan examined the card, which featured a picture of a Trandoshan male who was not wearing goggles and who had a heavily scarred muzzle. The name on the card was not Bossk's. The Sakiyan looked up at Bossk and said, 'Mundokk from Wasskah?'

'That's me, all right,' Bossk lied. 'The picture was taken before my scars healed, and before I lost my sight.' He patted Ezra's shoulder and added, 'This boy is my apprentice as well as my eyes.'

The Sakiyan said, 'Access to the DataCore is fifteen credits per hour or twenty-five credits per day.'

'We won't be long,' Bossk said. 'Boy, give the agent fifteen credits.'

Ezra had to resist the urge to glare at Bossk for making him pay with his own money. He reached into a jacket pocket and withdrew a small credit chip. The Sakiyan pointed to a slot in the transparisteel window, and Ezra pushed the chip through the slot. The Sakiyan said, 'You can use Console Five.'

Ezra led Bossk around the Ranat again and moved in front of Console Five. Ezra leant close to Bossk and whispered, 'You owe me fifteen credits.'

'Later,' Bossk said.

Bossk shifted his feet, adjusting his body to block Console Five from the view of the posting agent and the Ranat. 'Listen carefully, shorty. In case anyone's watching, move your fingers near the keypad as if you're searching for data, but let me do the work.' Bossk tilted his head so he didn't appear to be gazing directly at the monitor. 'First, I'm checking Imperial records for Lieutenant Herdringer, the guy who set me up.'

Ezra watched the console's monitor and drummed his fingers along the edges of the keypad while Bossk tapped at the keys. Ezra said, 'The licence that you showed to the agent. Who's Mundokk from Wasskah?'

'Someone who doesn't need his licence anymore,' Bossk said as he continued tapping at the keys.

An image of an Imperial officer with dark hair and a neatly trimmed moustache flickered onto the monitor. Text popped up in a window beside the image. Bossk looked at the readout and said, 'Well, I'll be blasted.'

'What's wrong?' Ezra said.

'Lieutenant Herdringer didn't set me up after all.'

'How do you know?'

'Because he died three months ago. Got hit by a speeder bus while crossing a street. Says so right on the screen.'

Confused, Ezra said, 'But you told me that you talked with Herdringer by holocomm before you landed on Lothal.'

'And now I'm telling you that the officer I talked with, the one who told me where to find Shifty Takkaro, wasn't Herdringer.'

'Maybe there's more than one Lieutenant Herdringer?'

'Not at the Imperial Security Bureau on Lothal,' Bossk said as he tapped again at the keypad.

Ezra said, 'What are you looking up now?'

'I want to know who replaced Herdringer at the Bureau,' Bossk said. The image of the moustached officer vanished from the monitor and was replaced by a blond officer. Bossk gnashed his teeth. 'Well, well. Say hello to Lieutenant Jenkes.'

Ezra looked at the flickering image and said, 'He's

the guy who claimed to be Herdringer?'

Bossk nodded. 'Yup. Arrived on Lothal just before Herdringer died.'

'Why would he lie to you?'

'Because he's hiding something, obviously,' Bossk said. He looked at the readout on Jenkes and scrolled through it. 'Says here, nine years ago, before Jenkes joined the Imperial service, he managed a gladiator arena on the planet Nyriaan.'

Ezra said, 'I wonder if he knows about the big fight on Lothal tonight.'

Bossk turned his head so he stared through his goggles at Ezra. 'What big fight?'

'I told you earlier. I was hired to sell tickets for it. Gamblers are coming from all over the galaxy to see the gladiators.'

'Gamblers and gladiators, huh?' Bossk muttered as he began tapping at the keypad again. The image of Jenkes vanished from the monitor and was replaced by a male Dug. Ezra recognised the Dug as the same one he'd seen at Ake's Tavern.

Data about the Dug named Gronson 'Shifty' Takkaro flowed onto the screen. Bossk scanned the data, then said, 'Shifty was a bookmaker at the gladiator arena on

Nyriaan at the same time Jenkes was there.'

Ezra said, 'You think they knew each other?'

Bossk let out a long hiss through his teeth. 'Yes, shorty. I think they knew each other.'

Lieutenant Jenkes was seated at his desk in his office at the Imperial Security Bureau when a warning light flashed on his computer console. He pressed a button and said, 'What is it?'

'Lieutenant Jenkes,' replied the RA-7 protocol droid. 'You said you wished to be notified if anyone searched your personal and military records on the Imperial Enforcement DataCore. I received an alert that your records are being accessed at a posting agency in the spaceport.'

Jenkes bit his lower lip. 'We have a security holocam in the posting agency?'

'Yes, Lieutenant. I'll get a visual now.' The RA-7 activated the holoprojector on Jenkes's console and a hologram of the posting agency's interior appeared. Although the flickering hologram did not clearly display each individual in the agency, Jenkes easily identified one figure as a caped Trandoshan wearing goggles.

'It's Bossk,' Jenkes said. 'Are any troops in the vicinity?'

'Yes, Lieutenant. Squad Three is across the street from the posting agency, at Imperial Substation 9K.'

'Notify Squad Three that the bounty hunter is a threat to Imperial security. And send reinforcements. The bounty hunter is to be shot on sight.'

'Yes, Lieutenant,' said the RA-7.

# CHAPTER 7
# PLAN B

**Still standing** beside Bossk in front of
Console Five inside the posting agency, Ezra said, 'OK,
so Lieutenant Jenkes and Shifty knew each other years
ago. But why did Jenkes lie to you about his name? And
why did those assassins try to kill you at Ake's Tavern?'

'We'll discuss that later,' Bossk said. 'Right now, we
gotta deal with the stormtoopers.'

Puzzled, Ezra said, 'What stormtroopers?'

'The ones about to come blasting their way in
here. You see, shorty, the problem with accessing the
Imperial Enforcement DataCore is that the Imperials
keep track of who accesses it and when. A guy like
Jenkes would keep track of such things, so he already
knows I'm here.' Bossk shoved his goggles up over his
forehead and turned to gaze past the Ranat and the
Nimbanel. He looked straight at the Sakiyan agent

seated behind the transparisteel window and asked him, 'Does this place have a back exit?'

The Sakiyan pointed to his left and said, 'Through that hallway.' Realising that the Trandoshan was making eye contact with him, the Sakiyan added, 'You told me you lost your sight.'

'I lied,' Bossk said as he pushed his cape back to reveal his mortar gun. He raised the gun and blasted the security holocam that was mounted to the ceiling, then swung the gun to aim it at the agency's entrance. Just as Bossk predicted, a stormtrooper came running in. Bossk fired a stun charge. The blast knocked the stormtrooper backwards and into another trooper directly behind him. Ezra jumped behind Bossk while the Ranat and Nimbanel took cover in the empty spaces between the computer consoles. Bossk fired once more at both troopers before he ran for the hallway. As Ezra ran after him, he saw the Sakiyan ducking down inside his booth.

Bossk held his mortar gun in front of him as he ran through the hallway. He rounded a corner where slit-like vertical windows lined a dark airshaft. Passing the airshaft, he slapped a button on the wall to open the back door. The door slid open and he ran outside and down a flight of steps that led into a narrow, steep-walled alley.

Ezra followed Bossk out the exit and into the alley. It turned sharply around a building and emptied into a slightly wider alley. Looking ahead, Ezra saw that it led to a side street. He saw people running past the mouth of the alley a moment before an amplified voice said, 'CLEAR THE STREETS IMMEDIATELY!'

Ezra was still running behind Bossk when he saw a stormtrooper appear at the end of the alley. Before the trooper could take aim, Bossk fired a stun charge. The trooper collapsed at the alley's mouth.

Bossk kept running and was about to jump over the fallen trooper when a rapid volley of laserfire smashed into the outer edges of the alley's walls. Bossk stopped short of the alley's mouth and Ezra almost ran into him. More laserfire tore into the walls, and then Ezra and Bossk heard the distinctive sound of approaching Imperial troop transports.

'Jenkes sent reinforcements,' Bossk muttered.

Outraged, Ezra said, 'You knew Jenkes would send troopers to the posting agency! Are you trying to get us killed?'

'I needed to find out who I'm dealing with,' Bossk said as he retreated into the alley. 'And if we get out of this alive, I also want to know more about the gladiator fight.' He went to a metal drainpipe that extended four storeys up to the building's roof. He slung his mortar gun over his shoulder, grabbed the pipe, and began scurrying up the side of the building.

Ezra followed Bossk, moving hand over hand up the pipe. Bossk reached the top and pulled himself onto the roof. Ezra was still climbing when he heard the report of a blaster rifle, and then red laserfire smashed into the pipe directly above his head. Ezra instinctively calculated the position of the stormtrooper who had just fired at him from below. He pressed his legs tightly against the pipe, holding himself in place long enough to use both hands to launch an energy ball from his slingshot. The energy ball sizzled down through the alley and met its mark, smashing into the trooper's helmet. Ezra returned his grip to the pipe but then he heard a horrid wrenching noise, and he realised the shattered pipe had broken away from the wall.

Clinging to the pipe, Ezra lurched backwards until he smacked against the opposite wall. He bent his knees and kicked off, launching himself up across the alley. His outstretched fingers connected with the edge of the roof, but he couldn't get a purchase. He gasped as his fingers began to slip from the roof's edge.

Bossk was perched just above Ezra. The Trandoshan

reached down fast and clamped one claw around Ezra's right wrist, preventing the boy from falling. Bossk yanked Ezra up beside him.

'Thanks,' Ezra said.

'Don't waste your breath,' Bossk said, 'just follow me.' He turned and ran across the roof, heading for its far side. He leapt from the roof over another alley, and landed on the roof of the neighbouring building.

Ezra realised Bossk was on top of the building that housed the posting agency. Against his better judgement, he ran and jumped to its roof and caught up with Bossk at the edge of a rectangular airshaft. Ezra looked down the shaft and saw that it was lined with slit windows and ventilation pipes, descending five floors. Ezra remembered passing the base of the shaft earlier. He said, 'You're not going back down there?'

'We need to get out of sight,' Bossk said. 'Do as I do.' He jumped down into the shaft. He landed on a ledge above a fifth-floor window and grabbed hold of a ventilation pipe to support himself.

Ezra considered leaving Bossk right there, but then he remembered Bossk's strongbox and the money it held. He jumped down into the shaft and landed on a ledge across from Bossk.

Bossk pressed himself close against the shaft's wall and motioned for Ezra to do the same. They heard footfalls on the first floor as stormtroopers followed their path to the posting agency's back door. After the stormtroopers had passed, Ezra opened his mouth to say something but Bossk glared at him and raised a single claw in front of his own mouth, signalling Ezra to remain silent.

Several seconds later, they heard the footsteps of two troopers walking on the first floor. Ezra realised that the stormtroopers were trailing the others, making sure they hadn't missed any important details. He also realised that Bossk was very familiar with how Imperial forces operated in the field.

After the two troopers passed, Bossk whispered, 'The troopers would never imagine we'd return to the posting agency.'

'So, what do we do now?'

'The gladiator fight that you mentioned. Where is it?'

'Monad Outpost. An abandoned mining facility about twenty kilometres out of the city. It has an old docking bay that's being used as an arena.'

'I don't imagine the local Imperials approve of

gladiator fights on Lothal. Do the fights happen often?'

'No. The only other one I know about was two months ago, at a different location. And it was so secret, I didn't hear about it until after it was over.'

'You said you were hired to sell tickets. Who hired you?'

Ezra hesitated before he said, 'A guy I know.'

'If this guy is a friend of yours, you should tell me about him because my gut says he could be in danger.'

'Danger? But how?'

Before Bossk could answer, a low humming noise came from below. Both Ezra and Bossk looked down and saw a small, spherical Imperial surveillance remote float through a first-floor window and into the shaft. The remote hovered to a stop at the bottom of the shaft and made a beeping noise before it emitted beams of light from its sensor arrays. The remote rotated, sending the beams in all directions, then began to slowly ascend.

Hoping to avoid detection, Ezra and Bossk sank back against the shaft's walls and froze. As the remote continued to rise, its beams struck the bottoms of the ledges beneath the windows and cast long, shifting shadows throughout the shaft. The remote was rising past the third-floor windows when Ezra looked at

Bossk. Bossk pointed to Ezra, tapped his own left wrist, and then pointed down.

Ezra understood Bossk's silent instruction. Moving carefully, he leant over the ledge and launched an energy ball from his slingshot. The ball smashed into the remote, shattering its metal surface. The remote exploded, spraying smoke and bits of fused metal and fried circuits throughout the shaft.

Ezra said, 'Mr Bossk, did plan B involve me blasting that remote?'

'Shut up and move,' Bossk said. He jumped down through the smoke, leaping from one ledge to another until he arrived at the bottom of the shaft.

Ezra followed him down. Bossk hooked his claws into the edges of one window and yanked it out of its frame. He set it on the shaft's floor before he stepped out of the shaft and into the hallway. Ezra stepped out after Bossk and said, 'Which way now?'

'The front door this time,' Bossk said as he pulled his goggles down over his eyes again. 'And we'll go out the same way we came in, with you leading the way.' He clamped one claw on Ezra's shoulder.

'But Mr Bossk, the stormtroopers may still be out –'

'Trust me, shorty,' Bossk said, and he shoved Ezra in

front of him. 'The stormtroopers have already scoured this building, but we gotta get out of here before they come looking for their remote. Just walk slowly, and no one will give us a second glance.'

As Ezra led Bossk through the hallway, Bossk made a slight adjustment to his cape so that it once again covered most of his upper body and also concealed his mortar gun. They returned to the main room of the posting agency, where they found the Ranat and Nimbanel engaged in conversation with the Sakiyan, who had stepped outside of his booth. Ezra heard them say the word 'Trandoshan.'

Ezra looked across the room to the front door and saw no sign of stormtroopers, including the ones that Bossk had stunned with his mortar gun. Ezra was suddenly aware of a thumping sensation, and he realised it came from his own heart, pounding in his chest.

Doing his best to remain calm and composed, Ezra walked with Bossk in tow, heading for the front door. As they passed the three aliens, the Ranat's long whiskers twitched and he turned his head to face Bossk. The Nimbanel and Sakiyan looked in Bossk's direction, too.

Bossk stopped walking and kept his grip on Ezra, forcing the boy to stop. Ezra wondered why Bossk had halted, and he looked at the other two bounty hunters. Both the Ranat and the Nimbanel had moved their hands close to the blasters that were holstered against their thighs.

'Don't do anything stupid,' Bossk said. 'I was set up by an Imperial officer, but I'm aiming to straighten everything out. I expect you to honour the Bounty Hunter Code and –'

The Ranat and Nimbanel moved fast for their weapons. Bossk moved faster. He swung his mortar gun out from under his cape and drove its barrel into the Nimbanel's stomach, then rapidly spun the gun to smash its stock into the Ranat's jaw. The Nimbanel doubled over while the Ranat's head bounced off the astonished Sakiyan's window. Bossk spun the mortar gun again, bringing the stock's trigger mechanism into his hand, and he fired a stun charge at the Nimbanel. Both the Ranat and the Nimbanel collapsed to the floor.

'Don't shoot!' said the Sakiyan as he raised his hands.

'So much for the Bounty Hunter Code,' Bossk said. 'Shorty, pull the helmet off that Nimbanel and give it to me.'

Ezra bent down beside the Nimbanel and began removing the large helmet. Bossk took off his own goggles, glared at the Sakiyan, and said, 'Why did these idiots try to blast me?'

Ezra said, 'Mr Bossk, look!' He pointed to the holograms projected above the computer consoles.

Bossk looked up at the holograms and saw that each one displayed a three-dimensional view of his head alongside personal data. 'Well, isn't that cute,' Bossk said. 'Lieutenant Jenkes placed a government bounty on me. I'm an official enemy of the Empire.'

'You don't sound very concerned,' Ezra said as he handed the Nimbanel's helmet to Bossk.

Bossk shrugged. 'I've been called worse.' He pulled the helmet over his head, then tapped a switch on its side, bringing its dark visor down over his face. He readjusted his cape over his body and mortar gun just as two stormtroopers came running through the front door.

Ezra expected Bossk to open fire on them, but he stood very still. The stormtroopers came to a stop in the centre of the room. Although Bossk's head was concealed by the Nimbanel's helmet and his cape covered his upper body and arms, his clawed toes remained exposed. Hoping to divert the stormtroopers' attention, Ezra said, 'Did you find the Trandoshan you're looking for?'

'Not yet,' one trooper replied. 'We sent a remote in here to search for any sign of him, but we lost the remote's signal. Did any of you see it?'

'I did,' Ezra said. 'It floated into an airshaft at the end of the hall, but then it exploded.' He gestured to the unconscious Nimbanel and Ranat. 'These two were standing near the airshaft when the explosion happened. We carried them in here. Maybe the Trandoshan is in the airshaft?'

The two stormtroopers took off, running for the hallway that led to the airshaft. Bossk raised his helmet's visor so the Sakiyan could see his face and said, 'The boy and I are leaving. If you send any troopers after us, trust that I'll live long enough to make you my last meal. Understand?'

The Sakiyan trembled but managed to nod his head in agreement.

Bossk lowered his visor and walked to the front door. Ezra caught up and said, 'I'm surprised you didn't blast those troopers.'

Bossk snorted. 'A good hunter knows when *not* to shoot. And look on the bright side. You don't have to play seeing-eye boy again.'

'I hope you won't mind my asking, Mr Bossk, but was your plan B an actual plan?'

'Plan B is all about staying alive,' Bossk said. 'I'm sticking with it.'

Outside the posting agency, they saw four stormtroopers standing between two Imperial Trooper Transporters. A few pedestrians moved past the buildings on the other side of the street but kept their distance from the stormtroopers. The stormtroopers looked at Bossk and Ezra but saw nothing suspicious about them and let them pass.

Ezra and Bossk continued walking. As they moved past a used landspeeder lot, Ezra said, 'Mr Bossk, back in the airshaft, you said the guy who hired me to sell tickets could be in danger. What makes you think that?'

Bossk stopped walking. Keeping his helmet's visor down, he faced Ezra and said, 'Consider the facts, shorty. Jenkes and Shifty knew each other by way of gladiator fights. Lieutenant Herdringer died shortly after Jenkes arrived on Lothal. And not long after that, a gladiator fight comes to Lothal, and another one is planned for tonight. Jenkes lied to me about his identity, set me up to get killed by three assassins at Ake's Tavern, and quite probably gave the order for the stormtroopers to try to kill me after the assassins failed. Shifty is dead. Now Jenkes has placed a bounty on me. I strongly suspect he's responsible for Herdringer's death, that he's involved with the gladiator fights, and that he'll kill anyone he thinks is a threat. If the guy who hired you to sell tickets to the fight is connected to Jenkes, he could be in deep trouble.'

Ezra sighed. 'I was hired by Ferpil Wallaway,' he said. 'He owns a pawn shop on the other side of the city. Ever since the Empire arrived on Lothal, there's been a lot of demand for black market goods. Ferpil buys and sells all sorts of stuff.' Ezra reached into his jacket pocket and pulled out the commlink component that he'd removed from the stormtrooper helmet. 'For example, I was going to sell him this commlink.'

'I don't care about commlinks,' Bossk said. 'How did Ferpil wind up selling tickets for the gladiator fights?'

'Someone called the Commissioner hired him. Ferpil sold tickets for the previous fight, too. That's how I found out about the fights, from Ferpil. The Commissioner has a hand in lots of criminal enterprises on Lothal, but I don't know anyone who's actually seen him or . . .' A sudden thought occurred to Ezra. 'Oh, wow. Do you think the Commissioner is really Lieutenant Jenkes?'

'Could be,' Bossk said. 'I want to talk with Ferpil. Where's he now?'

'Probably at his shop.'

'How far is that from here?'

'About nine kilometres. We could take the jump bike.'

'I'm through riding that heap,' Bossk said. 'We'll take a landspeeder.' He gestured to the used landspeeders parked in the lot. 'One of those should do.'

'You're buying a speeder?'

'No, shorty. I said we'll *take* one.'

'You lost the Trandoshan,' Lieutenant Jenkes said with dismay.

'Yes, Lieutenant,' replied the stormtrooper commander, who appeared as a hologram inside Jenkes's office. 'He took down several troops. Also destroyed a security holocam and one of our surveillance remotes. We're still searching the spaceport and concourse.'

'Find him and kill him!' Jenkes switched off the holocomm and looked at a chronometer. He went to his window. Looking out over the spaceport, he recalled that when Bossk had left the spaceport, he'd been accompanied by a boy. Jenkes hadn't received any updates on the boy since Bossk had fled the shootout at Ake's Tavern. He turned away from the window and pressed a button to summon his RA-7 protocol droid.

The office door slid open and the RA-7 walked in.

Jenkes said, 'I want to review holocam records from the spaceport this morning. Bossk left with a boy, and I want to see what that boy was up to before Bossk arrived.'

'Yes, Lieutenant,' said the RA-7. The droid nodded to Jenkes's console, and holograms appeared in the air. The hologram showed an isolated view of the spaceport at the moment Bossk and the boy were leaving together.

'Reverse the tape,' Jenkes said. The holograms of Bossk and the boy appeared to walk backwards to the landing pad where Bossk's ship rested. Keeping his eyes on the boy, Jenkes said to the droid, 'Increase speed on reverse until I tell you to stop.'

The figures appeared to move faster. Jenkes ignored Bossk walking backwards, and also the ship's reversed landing on Lothal, and continued to watch the boy. Minutes later, he saw a Xexto stop beside the boy. Jenkes said, 'Ferpil Wallaway.'

The RA-7 said, 'I beg your pardon, Lieutenant?'

'The Xexto is Ferpil Wallaway. He owns a pawn shop. He also deals with criminals.'

'You are far more knowledgeable about such things than I,' the droid said.

Jenkes rubbed his chin and mused aloud, 'I wonder how the boy is connected to Ferpil Wallaway.'

The droid was unsure if Jenkes had asked a question or expected a response, but the droid replied, 'I have no idea, Lieutenant.'

'Never mind,' Jenkes said. 'You're excused.'

The droid gave a slight bow, then turned and exited Jenkes's office. Jenkes continued watching Ferpil Wallaway and the boy, and noticed that they appeared to be friendly. He paused the tape and played it forwards to confirm that Wallaway had taken credit chips from the boy.

Jenkes switched off the datatape. He removed a compact datapad from his pocket to check the address of Ferpil Wallaway's pawn shop. He placed the datapad back in his pocket and looked around his office. He knew it would be the last time he ever saw the room.

Jenkes exited his office and stepped into the reception room where the black-metal RA-7 protocol droid stood beside a console and an open lift tube. The RA-7 turned its insectoid head to face Jenkes.

'Any updates?' Jenkes asked.

'No, Lieutenant.'

'I want an unmarked armoured speeder waiting for me in the Security hangar at once.'

'Will you require a driver, sir?'

'No.'

The droid nodded at a console and silently transmitted Jenkes's orders to the Security hangar. Mere seconds later, the droid faced Jenkes and said, 'The speeder is being moved to the hangar, Lieutenant. It will be ready momentarily.'

'I'll review messages when I return from my appointment.' Jenkes started walking towards the lift tube.

Confused, the RA-7 said, 'An appointment? But there's nothing listed on your itinerary.'

'It's not listed because it's classified.' Jenkes stopped in front of the lift tube and turned to face the RA-7. In his right hand, he held a compact blaster pistol. He fired the pistol, sending a laser bolt through the droid's head. The droid's metal arms reflexively reached up to the shattered remains of its head before its legs buckled, and it fell back across the reception room floor.

Jenkes pocketed his blaster pistol and stepped into the lift tube. The door slid shut behind him and the lift began its rapid descent to the hangar on the building's ground floor.

The lift came to a stop and the door slid open. Jenkes stepped out and found a bulky armoured landspeeder parked a short distance from a doorway that led to stormtrooper barracks. Two troopers stood beside the armoured speeder.

Jenkes faced the two troopers and said, 'You brought this vehicle out for me?'

'Yes, sir,' replied one trooper.

'You're both coming with me. Our mission is classified. Tell no one.'

'Yes, sir.'

The two troopers climbed into the armoured speeder with Jenkes. Jenkes got behind the controls and launched the speeder out of the hangar. He made his way onto a highway and headed for Ferpil Wallaway's shop.

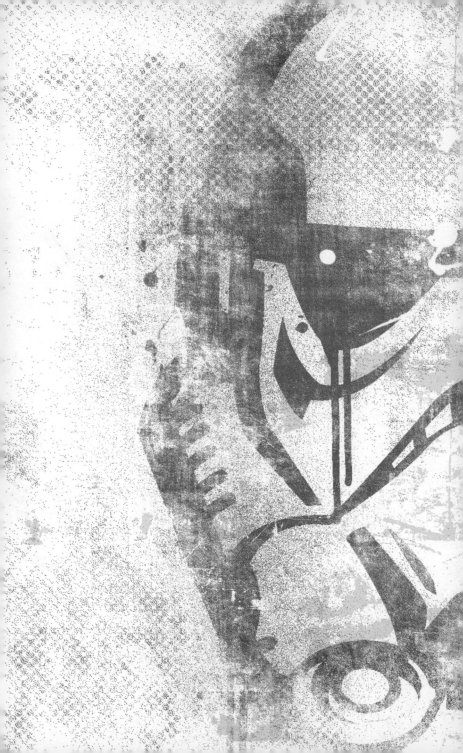

# CHAPTER 8
# THE PAWN SHOP

**'I've never seen** anyone boost a landspeeder so fast,' Ezra said. 'How'd you learn?'

'My father taught me,' Bossk said. He had wasted little time in stealing a dingy grey landspeeder with an enclosed cockpit and dark windows from the lot near the posting agency. The speeder's hood boasted a large spoiler, but Bossk drove only slightly over the city speed limit, easily manoeuvring the speeder through traffic on a highway that traversed the city. He was still wearing the helmet he'd taken from the Nimbanel but he'd raised the visor so he could see better through the speeder's windows.

Ezra said, 'Is your father a bounty hunter, too?'

'Yes,' Bossk hissed. He punched the speeder's accelerator and zipped in front of an open speeder bus that carried a family of tentacled aliens. The speeder bus's driver honked at Bossk and shook a tentacle angrily.

Ezra said, 'Did your father teach you how to drive, too?'

Bossk hissed again. 'If you don't ask me any more pesky questions about my father, I won't ask about yours.'

The comment stung Ezra. He looked away from Bossk and stared out the window.

Bossk chuckled. 'Take it from me, kid. Fathers are overrated.'

Wanting to change the subject, Ezra said, 'Could you teach me to boost a landspeeder?'

'Not unless you grew claws.'

Ezra drummed his fingers on the speeder's black dashboard. 'I still think you should have stolen the red one. That model looked more powerful than this one.'

Bossk snorted in disgust. 'I already told you, shorty. On most worlds, if you want to blend in with the environment, your best bet is to steal a speeder that's dark grey or a dusty-looking green. If you steal a red speeder, you might as well send out invitations asking the police to chase you down.'

'But what if you're on a planet where everything is mostly red?'

'Mostly red?' Bossk snorted again. 'Are you mocking me?'

'Absolutely not, Mr Bossk. I'm just curious.'

'Have you ever been to a "mostly red" planet before?'

'No,' Ezra said. 'I've never been off Lothal.'

'That explains a lot,' Bossk muttered.

'Turn right up ahead,' Ezra said, 'and then take the next exit.'

Bossk followed Ezra's instructions, steering the speeder to leave the highway and travel down a ramp that led to an old commercial district. Lothal's sun had begun to set, so Bossk switched on the speeder's running lights. A few seconds later, streetlights automatically winked on.

Ezra said, 'Go straight two blocks, then turn right.'

Wallaway's Pawn Shop was on the first floor of a two-storey ferrocrete building located on the corner of a block that also included an agricultural supply store, a wholesale food market, and a salvage yard. The pawn shop was identified by angular illuminated letters that were set above the establishment's front door. It was next to a wide window that displayed an assortment of tools, musical instruments, old clothes, and unusual appliances. Across the street from the pawn shop was the Go-Lothal Hotel, a derelict complex of connected domed structures.

Bossk slowed down and proceeded to glide past Ferpil's shop. Ezra said, 'You went right by it! Where are you going?'

'I'm circling the block,' Bossk said.

'Why?'

'Because bounty hunters do things like that, stupid.'

Bossk's eyes flicked back and forth, scanning the streets, buildings, and other vehicles as he guided the grey speeder around the block. He was wrapping around the last corner when he spotted an armoured landspeeder parked to the side of the Go-Lothal Hotel. He said, 'We got company.'

Ezra said, 'Huh? Where?'

Bossk pointed to the armoured speeder. Ezra said, 'Imperial?'

'Yes,' Bossk hissed. He brought the grey speeder to a stop alongside a curb fifteen metres away from the armoured speeder.

Ezra said, 'What do we do now?'

'We wait and watch for a minute. Maybe two.'

Worried about Ferpil, Ezra squirmed in his seat. He

said, 'What if Ferpil needs our help?'

'And what if we're already too late?' Bossk said. 'We're not getting out of this speeder or barging in anywhere until I have some idea of what we're up against.'

Looking at the pawn shop's windows, Ezra saw a brief burst of light from within. 'Mr Bossk, did you –?'

'I saw it, too,' Bossk said.

A shadowy form of a man moved away from the pawn shop's side door. The man was carrying a large luggage case. He walked towards the parked armoured speeder. As he passed under a streetlight, the man was revealed as a blond human who wore an Imperial officer's uniform.

'Jenkes,' Bossk said as he removed a small disc-shaped device from his belt.

Ezra watched Jenkes climb into the armoured speeder. He shouted, 'Do something, Mr Bossk! Before he gets away!'

'Quiet!' Bossk said as he opened the grey landspeeder's cockpit canopy. Moving carefully, Bossk extended his arm so it dangled along the side of the gray speeder, then he jerked his arm forwards and whipped his wrist, sending the disc skipping on its edge along the street. It rolled straight under the armoured speeder before it leapt up and secured itself to the speeder's metal underside. The armoured speeder launched away from the curb, taking the disc with it.

Ezra said, 'What did you do?'

'Planted a magnetic tracer beacon on his speeder so we can follow him later,' Bossk said. He lowered his helmet's visor before he climbed out of the landspeeder. Ezra got out after him. They walked across the street and went to the side door of Ferpil's shop.

The door was open. They walked in. The shop was filled with shelves constructed from scrap metal. The shelves were cluttered with small items for sale. A long table that had been transformed into a workbench extended from one wall. On top of the workbench was an empty cash box.

Bossk's nostrils flared at the scent of blaster gas.

They found Ferpil sprawled on the floor behind the workbench. A thin trail of smoke was still rising from his chest where the blaster bolt had hit him. Two of his six arms were bent underneath his body. His eyes were closed but Ezra saw his mouth twitch.

Bossk squatted down beside Ferpil's body while Ezra dropped to his knees and cupped his hand behind the Xexto's small head. 'Ferpil! Ferpil, it's me, Ezra!'

Ferpil's left eye opened slightly. Bossk said, 'The man who shot you. Is he the Commissioner?'

'Yes,' Ferpil gasped. 'Never saw him before. But he told me . . . he's the Commissioner. He came for his credits. He . . . he didn't have to . . .' Ferpil's eye closed and his body went slack.

Ezra shouted, 'Ferpil!'

'He's gone, kid,' Bossk said.

Ezra glared at the Trandoshan. 'If we'd got out of the landspeeder instead of waiting, Ferpil would still be alive.'

Bossk rose to his feet. 'Don't blame yourself.'

'I'm not! I'm blaming you!'

Bossk reached down, grabbed the front of Ezra's jacket, and lifted the boy up so he was standing. Ezra jerked out of Bossk's grip but continued glaring at him.

Bossk pulled the helmet off his head and held it at his side. 'Listen,' he said. 'If we'd walked in here sooner, Jenkes might have killed you, too. Maybe he would have got both of us. Maybe his armoured landspeeder was loaded with stormtroopers just waiting to blast us away. But I strongly advise you to stop wondering about how things might have happened differently, and suggest we focus on getting the man who killed Ferpil.'

Ezra looked down at Ferpil's corpse. Bossk said, 'I'm low on ammo. Did Ferpil keep any on the premises?'

'Back room,' Ezra said, and gestured to a doorway behind him. 'In the cupboard on the left.'

Bossk went into the back room. Ezra looked at the empty cash box. Bossk returned, carrying his helmet, which he'd stuffed with several ammo packs.

Ezra pointed to the cash box and said, 'Jenkes couldn't wait until after the fight to collect his money. I'm guessing that after he learnt you'd looked up his data at the posting agency, he got scared. So he decided to make a run for it and to take as much money with him as he could.'

'As long as you're making guesses,' Bossk said as he reloaded his mortar gun, 'what's your guess about Jenkes's next move?'

'He's going to the arena at Monad Outpost. Because that's where the big money is. With the gamblers.'

Bossk reached to the side of his belt and removed a small oval-shaped scanner. He thumbed the scanner's lid open, activated the device, and saw a winking red blip appear on the scanner's tiny monitor. He said, 'Is Monad Outpost south-west of the city?'

'Yes,' Ezra said.

'Then you guessed right. Come on.'

'What about Ferpil?'

'What about him?' Bossk stepped over Ferpil's corpse and walked fast towards the side door.

Ezra took a last look at the dead Xexto before he hurried after Bossk. They returned to the grey landspeeder, Bossk started the engine, and they raced off, heading for Monad Outpost.

'Good evening, fight fans, and welcome to Gladiator Night at Monad Arena,' said a female Pa'lowick who stood on a small, hovering platform in the middle of the open-roofed former docking bay. 'Are you ready to meet the gladiators?'

The spectators roared in anticipation. Over five thousand people had squeezed onto the recently installed cheap metal seats that encircled the arena's central pit. The seats bounced up and down under the enthusiastic crowd. Among the spectators were people who had purchased tickets from Ezra, including the long-horned Chagrian who sat in a luxury box with his four Twi'lek companions.

The Pa'lowick rolled her bulbous eyes and leant her long snout, which ended with a pair of large lips, into the comlink that was mounted to her floating platform. She made a smacking noise with her lips, and loudspeakers transformed the noise into a cracking echo throughout the arena. 'Mmm-mmm!' she said as her body wiggled atop her long, thin legs. 'I can hardly wait for this fight to get going either. But first, allow me to remind you good people that if you haven't already placed your bets, now is the time!'

The Chagrian shouted, 'I've placed my bets! Get on with the fight!' The four Twi'leks in his box smiled and applauded as if their host had said something remarkably witty.

Ignoring the Chagrian, the Pa'lowick said, 'Before we begin, I'd also like to remind you that this event is not authorised by any local authorities. If you want to see more gladiator fights on Lothal, and I'm guessing you do . . .'

Another loud round of applause came from the spectators.

'. . . be sure to keep the fights our little secret!'

As the Pa'lowick continued her banter, an unmarked armoured Imperial landspeeder arrived at the edge of a wide parking area outside the arena at Monad Outpost. Lieutenant Jenkes was seated in the landspeeder's cockpit. The two stormtroopers that he'd brought from the Security building stood in the compartment behind him. The parking area was filled with hundreds of vehicles, including a large number of privately owned speeder buses that had brought many spectators to Monad Outpost.

Jenkes steered past rows of parked vehicles and brought the armoured speeder to a stop next to an old garage that jutted from the side of the arena. He exited the armoured speeder and the two stormtroopers followed, taking their blaster rifles with them. Standing outside the speeder, Jenkes faced the stormtroopers and said, 'I received a report about an illegal gladiator fight and gambling at this location. Judging from the number of vehicles in the lot, it appears the event has attracted many unsavoury types. I'm determined to find out who's responsible for this outrage, and ensure that it never happens on Lothal again.'

Inside the arena, thousands of spectators cheered at the same time, producing a noise so loud that the two stormtroopers could feel it in their bones. The stormtroopers looked at each other, then turned their helmets to face Jenkes. One trooper said, 'Sir, shouldn't we call for backup?'

'And risk revealing that Imperial forces were oblivious to a league of criminals setting up this event? No, we'll handle this ourselves. An informant provided me with instructions for where to find this event's box office, where the fight organisers will no doubt be counting their profits. We shall arrest them and bring them back to the city.'

'Yes, sir,' the stormtrooper replied with an uncertain tone.

The troopers followed Jenkes into the garage. He led them into a lift tube that ascended to a long corridor that was illuminated by old tubular glow rods that dangled from dusty cables on the ceiling. Jenkes said, 'According to my informant, this corridor leads directly to the box office.'

As Jenkes and the troopers proceeded down the hall, they heard an incredible roar that caused the walls to shake. Jenkes guessed that the gladiators had just entered the arena.

'Presenting Borbig Drob the Houk!' announced the female Pa'lowick to the arena crowd. 'Nine-time champion of the Stormblade Bloodfest!'

The heavily muscled Houk lumbered into the arena, carrying a heavy sword and a broad shield. Thousands of spectators cheered and booed him.

'And presenting the challenger,' the Pa'lowick continued, 'Warjak the Feeorin! Undefeated champion of the Outer Rim Carve-up!'

The Feeorin shook his thick tendrils as he strode into the arena, carrying a massive vibro-axe and a stun net. Again, the spectators loudly voiced either their admiration or contempt. Some spectators threw small weapons into the arena. Others threw raw meat and rotten fruit.

The Pa'lowick guided her floating platform away from the two gladiators and hovered near a doorway that led to the box office. The Houk and the Feeorin walked to the centre of the arena and faced each other. Neither bowed. Speaking low enough so only the Houk could hear, the Feeorin said, 'Remember, the Commissioner will pay us a fortune if I win.'

'I remember,' the Houk said as he raised his sword.

And the battle began.

# CHAPTER 9
# GLADIATOR NIGHT

# 'There's Monad Outpost,'

Ezra said.

'Big place,' Bossk said. Through the stolen grey landspeeder's windscreen, they saw hundreds of speeders parked outside the abandoned mining complex's largest docking bay. Lothal's moons were in the night sky, bathing the area in reflected sunshine.

Bossk glanced at his compact scanner and said, 'The tracer beacon's signal is coming from over there, next to that garage.' He increased power to the landspeeder's thrusters, raced over the parking lot, and brought the speeder to a shuddering stop a short distance from the armoured speeder. He picked up the helmet that held the ammo packs that he'd taken from Ferpil's shop and handed the helmet to Ezra. 'Carry this and stay close to me,' Bossk said, 'in case I run out of ammo.' He grabbed his mortar gun as he climbed out of the grey speeder.

'But what if the Imperials or another bounty hunter sees you?' Ezra said as he followed Bossk into the garage. 'Shouldn't you be wearing the helmet?'

'I'm done with disguises for the day, shorty. When we catch up with Jenkes, I want to see the look on his face when he sees mine.'

As they entered the garage's lift tube and ascended to a dimly lit corridor, Ezra said, 'I hate to say so, Mr Bossk, but I have a bad feeling about this.'

Jenkes led the two stormtroopers to a right-angled turn in the corridor, which brought them into a shorter corridor that ended with a closed door. 'Here's the box office,' Jenkes said. He pushed a wall switch and the door slid open. The troopers followed him into the room.

Inside, Jenkes and the troopers found an Ishi Tib, a green-skinned humanoid amphibian with a beak-like mouth and large eyes that extended from angular stalks on either side of his head. The Ishi Tib held a datapad and stood before a computer bank. Next to the computer bank, a row of three repulsorlift carts supported the weight of over three dozen large bins that were filled with credit chips.

The Ishi Tib looked up from his datapad, saw Jenkes with the two stormtroopers, and his beak opened in surprise. Jenkes pulled out his compact blaster pistol, aimed it at the Ishi Tib, and said, 'Do you work for the Commissioner?'

'I . . . I don't know what you're talking about,' the Ishi Tib stammered as he lowered his datapad.

Jenkes shot the Ishi Tib in the chest. The Ishi Tib collapsed against the computer bank and then slumped to the floor. The stormtroopers didn't flinch.

Jenkes turned to the troopers and said, 'I thought he was reaching for a weapon.' He looked at the carts loaded with credit chips. 'If we really want to deal a blow to these criminals, we should confiscate their haul now. We'll take these carts to the speeder. Now.'

'Yes, sir.' Each trooper grabbed a cart, then pushed it through the air to the door.

Jenkes grabbed the remaining cart and followed the troopers out of the room. He still carried his blaster pistol. Although it was a small weapon, it was powerful enough to pierce stormtrooper armour. Jenkes planned on using it for that precise purpose after the troopers loaded the credits into the armoured speeder.

Ezra and Bossk had just walked around the right-angled turn in the corridor when a door slid open in front of them and a stormtrooper emerged, pushing a repulsorlift cart that carried bins of credit chips. Bossk saw a second trooper and Lieutenant Jenkes moving behind the first trooper. Without any hesitation, Bossk raised his mortar gun and fired at the first trooper.

The blast knocked the trooper backwards into the cart behind him, which smashed into the second trooper. Bossk kept his eyes focused on Jenkes as he fired again, hitting the second trooper and causing Jenkes to let out a loud yelp as he jumped back into the room, taking cover behind a computer terminal. Both troopers fell, and Bossk ran for the open doorway.

'Wait for me!' Ezra said as he ran after Bossk, carrying the helmet that held the ammo packs. Bossk had almost reached the doorway when Jenkes opened fire from behind the computer console. A laser bolt whizzed past Bossk and Ezra, and Jenkes fired again. The second laser bolt zipped through Bossk's cape, passing through the gap between his left arm and ribcage. Bossk and Ezra threw their bodies against two narrow partitions on either side of the doorway to avoid getting hit.

'It's all over, Jenkes!' Bossk said. 'I know you're the Commissioner!'

'I don't know what you're talking about,' Jenkes called back.

'Don't play any games with me,' Bossk said. 'You were Shifty's partner. When I came after him, you decided to have us both killed, so you could keep all the money.'

Several seconds of silence passed before Jenkes replied, 'We're both businessmen, bounty hunter. There's a lot of credits at stake. Plenty for both of us. If you help me get it back to the spaceport, I'll –'

'You'll what?' Bossk interrupted. 'Take the bounty off my head and give me half the money?'

'Yes!' Jenkes said. 'I can do that!'

'I'm not so sure you can,' Bossk said. 'You see, scum like you would sooner blast me like you did Ferpil Wallaway, or shove me in front of a speeder bus, the same way you killed Herdringer.'

'How'd you know I killed Herdringer?'

'I didn't until you just admitted it, lamebrain,' Bossk said. 'But if I'm going to clear my name, I may need you alive, so I'll make a deal. Surrender by the count of three, and I won't toss a thermal detonator in there. One!'

'Wait! I'll –'

'Two.'

Ezra and Bossk heard footfalls. Ezra said, 'He's running away! Use the thermal detonator!'

'I don't have one on me,' Bossk said. 'I was bluffing.' He jumped over the fallen stormtroopers and ran into the box office with his mortar gun in front of him.

Ezra followed him in and saw the dead Ishi Tib sprawled beside the computer bank. Ezra moved past the computer bank and said, 'There's another corridor. He must have run this way. Come on!'

Bossk ran after Ezra. They turned a corner that led to a long stairwell. As they ran down the stairs, they heard an incredibly loud roar from the crowd within the arena. Ezra said, 'We must be getting close to the gladiator fight.'

A door was at the bottom of the stairs. Bossk reached the door first. The door opened automatically and Ezra followed Bossk through the doorway.

They were in the arena. To Ezra's left, a female Pa'lowick stood on a floating platform. Directly in front of him, a large Feeorin was swinging a vibro-axe at a Houk who carried a huge sword. And beyond the two gladiators, thousands of spectators were standing atop their seats, shaking their fists in excitement and yelling as loud as they could.

Ezra had never seen a gladiator fight before and was momentarily dumbstruck.

Bossk looked to his right and spotted Jenkes running alongside the base of the wall that curved around the arena floor. The spectators were so focused on the gladiators that few seemed to notice the Imperial officer. Bossk raised his mortar gun and aimed at Jenkes but immediately realised he'd emptied his last rounds on the two stormtroopers. He looked at Ezra, saw the boy staring at the gladiators, and shouted, 'Stop daydreaming! Throw me a stun cartridge!'

Ezra reached into the helmet he was carrying, pulled out a cartridge, and tossed it to Bossk. The cartridge was still arcing through the air when a laser bolt tore through the side of Bossk's right thigh. Bossk hissed as he dropped his gun and fell to the arena floor, clutching at his leg.

Ezra turned to see who had shot the laser bolt. He saw Jenkes, both hands gripping a small blaster pistol.

Jenkes's shooting had attracted the attention of many spectators, and they let out a collective gasp at the sight of an Imperial officer within the arena. Within seconds, a stunned silence swept over the crowd. The gladiators continued fighting until they also became aware of the sudden quiet. The Houk and the Feeorin pulled away from each other and looked at the Imperial officer, and then noticed the human boy who stood near a Trandoshan, not far from the hovering Pa'lowick.

The Pa'lowick looked from Bossk to Jenkes, then pushed her lips close to her commlink and said, 'Last I checked, folks, this is a gladiator fight, not a shooting gallery!'

Hearing the Pa'lowick over the loudspeakers, many spectators responded with nervous laughter. Jenkes kept his blaster aimed at Bossk as he walked fast across the arena floor. As he walked past Ezra and Bossk, he picked up Bossk's mortar gun before he proceeded to the Pa'lowick's platform. When he was just below the Pa'lowick, he said, 'Give me that comlink. Now. Before I have you shot.'

Intimidated, the Pa'lowick bent her thin legs and stooped on her platform to hand the comlink to Jenkes. Keeping his blaster aimed at Bossk, Jenkes took the comlink, faced the audience, and said, 'I'm Lieutenant Jenkes of the Imperial Security Bureau. Monad Outpost is completely surrounded by Imperial troops. This Trandoshan is a criminal, wanted for crimes against the Empire.'

The spectators murmured anxiously. Ezra glanced at Bossk and whispered, 'Mr Bossk! I'm still carrying the comlink that I took from the stormtrooper helmet.'

'And?' Bossk asked.

'I think it's about time the local authorities learnt what Jenkes has been up to,' said Ezra. Moving carefully so Jenkes couldn't see what he was doing, he removed the comlink from his jacket pocket, set it for long-range transmission, and activated it.

Still facing the spectators, Jenkes continued, 'The Empire has no interest in this gladiator fight or the spectators in attendance. We only want the Trandoshan. And we want him . . . dead.'

Some spectators gasped. Others, eager to see blood, shouted their approval. Bossk looked at Ezra and said, 'Your comlink's on?'

Ezra nodded.

'Hold on!' Bossk bellowed loud enough that several hundred spectators could hear him. He raised his claws to show he held no weapons, and then he lowered one claw to push himself up from the floor. Wobbling on his wounded leg, he shouted, 'I am Bossk from Trandosha! I did not come to Monad Outpost to die in this arena. But if I am to die tonight, I wish to die as a warrior. I challenge the gladiators to bare-handed combat!'

The response from the spectators was an overwhelming wave of shouts and screams. Before Jenkes could protest, Bossk limped towards the Houk and the Feeorin, who gazed at him as if he were out of his mind. He came to a stop about a metre away from them, held his arms out by his sides, and said, 'Come on, fellas. Give a dead guy a break. Bare-handed means bare-handed.' He grimaced as he shifted his weight onto his good leg.

The Houk and the Feeorin looked at each other and grinned. They looked back at Bossk and released their grips on their weapons.

Before the Houk's sword hit the ground, Bossk launched himself off his good leg, straight for the Houk. Bossk's forehead smashed into the Houk's face as he grabbed the Houk's forearms and drove his knee into his gut. The Houk fell back with Bossk on top of him. Bossk pushed himself off, flipping his body back at the startled Feeorin.

Bossk's right claw raked across the Feeorin's chest. The Feeorin snarled as he tumbled to the ground, but when he came up standing, he was holding the Houk's sword. He swung the sword at Bossk. Bossk ducked, and as the blade whooshed over his head, he said, 'That's not bare-handed!'

Bossk bent down on his good leg and kicked out with his bad. He grunted as his wounded leg struck the side of the Feeorin's shin so hard that one of the Feeorin's bones snapped. The Feeorin wailed as he crumpled to the floor. Bossk spat at him and said, 'I hate cheaters.'

The Feeorin passed out next to the Houk. Bossk rose to his feet. He looked at Jenkes, who still had his blaster pistol aimed at Bossk. Bossk shifted his gaze to Ezra, who held up the small comlink component to show Bossk that it was still transmitting. Finally, Bossk turned to face the spectators.

'Now that I have your attention,' Bossk said, 'I am Bossk of the Bounty Hunters Guild. Lieutenant Jenkes is really the Commissioner, the man responsible for arranging this fight. Jenkes is also guilty of the murder of Lieutenant Herdringer of the Imperial Security Bureau, the pawnbroker Ferpil Wallaway, an Ishi Tib in this building, and probably a bunch of other people. And he tried to have some assassins kill me, and placed a bounty on my head under false pretenses.'

The spectators gazed at Bossk in astonishment.

'Oh, I almost forgot,' Bossk continued. 'Jenkes also attempted to steal all the credit chips that you hard-working citizens brought here tonight.'

Although Jenkes held a blaster pistol and also carried Bossk's mortar gun, outraged spectators began throwing whatever they could grab at him. Jenkes tapped the controls of the repulsorlift platform and raced for the door to the stairway that led back to the box office.

Ezra raised his slingshot and launched an energy bolt at Jenkes. The bolt struck Jenkes's head and he fell backwards off the platform, dropping his pistol and Bossk's gun before landing hard on the arena floor. The hovering platform veered off course and crashed into the wall beside the door.

Jenkes groaned but didn't move. Bossk limped over to him and placed one foot on top of his body. Then he clenched his fists and raised them defiantly high above his head. The spectators began chanting, 'Bossk! Bossk! Bossk!'

The Pa'lowick turned her bulbous eyes to face Ezra and said, 'Now *that* guy really knows how to put on a show.'

And then the Imperial forces arrived at the outpost and swarmed the arena.

# CHAPTER 10
# THE STRONG BOX

**The morning** after the big fight, Ezra stood across the street from the Imperial Security Bureau, keeping his eyes on the building's main entrance. From where he was standing, he couldn't help overhearing the voice of the HoloNet News reporter, broadcasting from a speaker built into the cart of a nearby food vendor.

'Last night,' the reporter said, 'an illegal sporting event at Monad Outpost on Lothal might have ended in civilian casualties if not for the courageous actions of Bossk the Trandoshan, a prominent member of the Bounty Hunters Guild. Bossk had been stalking a fugitive on Lothal when he became aware of an underworld crime syndicate's scheme to lure gamblers from across the galaxy to Monad Outpost. In other news . . .'

Ezra stopped listening to the broadcast when he saw Bossk step out of the security building. Bossk was still limping, but only slightly. He walked over to Ezra and said, 'Hey, shorty. What brings you here?'

'We had a deal, Mr Bossk,' Ezra said. 'Remember? The strongbox?'

'Oh, that,' Bossk said. 'Sure, I remember. You're probably as eager to get that strongbox as I am to leave this planet. Come on, walk me to my ship.'

They began walking across the concourse, heading for the landing pad where Bossk had left *Hound's Tooth*. Ezra said, 'Your name was on the HoloNet News. The Empire is making you out to sound like a real hero. They called you 'courageous.''

Bossk made a hacking noise, chuckling. 'I kind of insisted that they call me that. After everything Jenkes put me through, I deserve some good publicity from the Empire. Also, they appreciated the fact that I only fired my mortar gun in self-defence, and that I used stun charges when I shot at the troopers.'

'I noticed the news didn't mention Jenkes.'

Bossk shrugged. 'No surprise there. The Empire never generates bad publicity about itself.'

'So, what happened to Jenkes?' Ezra said. 'Is he

going to prison?'

'Let's just say you'll never hear of him again. Ever. I got that guarantee from two Imperial officers, Commandant Aresko and Taskmaster Grint.'

'And you trusted them?'

'After I explained everything Jenkes did, including killing Ferpil, the Imperials decided to pay me for all my hard work on Lothal. I only came here to get Shifty Takkaro but wound up making quite a profit.'

They arrived at the landing pad. Bossk said, 'Wait here.' Ezra stood at the edge of the pad while Bossk entered his ship. Less than a minute later, Bossk returned, carrying a small metal box. 'Here you go, shorty. It's all yours.'

Ezra took the metal box and opened it. The box contained three small credit chips. Ezra examined the chips. 'These . . . these are worth just seventy-five credits.'

'And they're all yours.'

'Seventy-five credits,' Ezra repeated. 'That's it?'

'You expected more?'

'You . . . you tricked me!'

'Let's backtrack, shorty. I said that if you helped me, I'd give you all the money in my strongbox. Did I not hold up my end of the bargain?'

'That wasn't any bargain,' Ezra said through clenched teeth. 'That was a swindle!'

Bossk winced. 'It's not like we had a written contract or anything.'

'I saved your life! I . . . I helped you get into the posting office! I . . . You . . . You still owe me fifteen credits from the posting office!'

'Right, I forgot,' Bossk said. He reached into a pocket, pulled out a credit chip, and handed it to Ezra. 'See, that's not so bad. Now you have ninety credits.'

Ezra scowled. 'Lucky me.'

'I'd give you more if I could, just as a favour, but I'm short on hard currency. The Empire prefers to pay bounty hunters by transfer register.'

Two stormtroopers approached Bossk and Ezra. The stormtroopers walked on either side of a long plastoid box that rested on a repulsorlift cart. The troopers brought the cart to a stop in front of Bossk, and one trooper said, 'For you. From Commandant Aresko.'

The troopers turned and walked away, leaving the cart and long box.

Ezra looked at the box on the cart and said, 'Short on hard currency, huh? So, tell me, what's inside *that* box?'

Bossk's mouth twisted into an ugly smile, and then he answered, 'Jenkes.'

'Oh,' Ezra said.

'So long, shorty,' Bossk said. 'It's been fun.' He shoved the floating cart towards his ship's boarding hatch.

Ezra stowed the small metal strongbox in his backpack. He turned away from the landing pad and started making his way for the exit. He had no desire to hang around the spaceport or watch Bossk's ship lift off. He just wanted to go home.

Ezra plodded across the plains, heading for the abandoned tower. It wasn't until he cleared a rise and could see the tower's silhouette on the horizon that he remembered that he'd left his jump bike in the city. He decided to recover it later.

He heard a high-pitched noise from somewhere overhead, and instantly recognised the distinct sound of an Imperial TIE fighter. As the noise grew louder, he determined it was approaching from behind him. He stopped and turned, swinging his gaze up at the sky. He quickly spotted the TIE fighter, moving fast after another ship, a mid-sized diamond-shaped freighter.

The freighter zoomed overhead, and the TIE stayed on its tail. The TIE opened fire on the freighter, and

Ezra winced as laserfire struck the freighter's shields. He doubted that the freighter could evade the nimble TIE, so he was extremely surprised when the freighter ascended rapidly and looped back so it was directly behind the TIE. The freighter opened fire, blasting the unshielded TIE's cockpit. A moment later, the freighter peeled off and ascended into the clouds.

Ezra shifted his gaze back to the TIE, which was trailing fire as it angled down over the plains. The TIE barely cleared a distant hill before it appeared to vanish over the high grass.

Ezra's eyes widened as he heard the TIE crash. Without any thought of his own safety, he bolted across the ground, running towards the dark smoke that billowed up from beyond the hill.

He was breathing hard when he finally crested the hill. The TIE had crashed in the middle of a wide field, and the smoke was rising from the fighter's shattered cockpit. Ezra glanced around and noted that not a single structure or vehicle was visible. He smiled.

He raced down the hill and onto the field. Reaching the TIE, he scrambled up onto the side of the spherical cockpit, keeping his face and hands away from the smoke. He swung himself towards the cracked canopy and saw the black-helmeted pilot still strapped into his seat. Ezra shouted, 'Mister!'

The pilot shuddered.

Ezra said, 'Hey, you OK? You alive?'

'Get your hands off my craft!' the pilot snapped, his voice filtering through his helmet's speaker. 'This fighter is property of the Empire!'

Ezra smiled ruefully, then muttered, 'Guess that's a yes.' He shifted his hands on the cockpit's laser-scorched hull, which was almost too hot to touch, and noticed the cockpit was filling up with smoke.

The pilot shifted in his seat and hit an emergency switch to open the canopy. The canopy popped open, but only by a few millimetres. Ezra realised the canopy's opening mechanisms had jammed.

The pilot began coughing. Ezra grabbed hold of the lip of the cockpit and swung his body up. He landed just behind the pilot and the partially raised canopy. The pilot struggled against his seat as he tried to turn his helmeted head to look up at Ezra through the smoke. The pilot said, 'I told you to get off this ship!'

Ezra stuck his fingers into the gap between the canopy and cockpit. 'Not much of a ship anymore,' he said. 'Besides, I'm just trying to open her up –'

The canopy snapped open and smoke poured out from the cockpit. The pilot coughed as he removed his helmet. Able to turn his head more freely, he looked up at Ezra, and for a moment, Ezra thought the pilot's expression looked grateful. But then the pilot's face hardened. Ezra said, 'Hey, don't say thank you or anything.'

The pilot sneered. 'Thank you? I'm an Officer of the Imperial Navy. I didn't need your help.'

Ezra grinned. 'Course not.'

The pilot began to rise, but Ezra pushed down on his shoulder and said, 'Wait! Your sleeve's caught on the flight recorder.'

'It is?'

'Let me just unhook it for you,' Ezra said as he extended a hand behind the back of the pilot's seat. But his fingers never touched the cockpit's flight recorder, and instead he grabbed a transceiver calibration plug, which he quickly stuffed into his backpack.

The pilot said, 'What was that?'

Ignoring the question, Ezra said, 'So, why were you chasing that cargo ship? Were they smugglers?'

Making another effort to rise, the pilot said, 'That's confidential infor –'

'Whoa, there, sir,' Ezra said as he pushed the pilot back down again. 'Bit of metal caught on your, um, posterior.' Leaning deeper into the cockpit, he added,

'Wouldn't want an Officer of the Imperial Navy to split his pants.'

'No, I—'

'That just wouldn't be dignified. Hold still, now.' Ezra reached behind the pilot's seat again. 'Almost got it. . . . There!' He plucked a diagnostic uplink port switch, shoved it into his backpack, and pushed himself out from the cockpit. 'Now remember, sir. No thank-yous.'

The pilot, clutching his helmet, began to rise from his seat. Still positioned above him, Ezra said, 'Here, I'll take that.' He reached down and took the helmet, allowing the pilot to use both hands to pull himself out of the cockpit. 'You didn't need my help, and besides . . . I didn't come to help.'

Ezra moved fast. He placed both feet on top of the pilot's bare head, and then kicked off, launching himself away from the TIE fighter and taking the helmet with him. He somersaulted down and hit the ground running. 'Just came to score a little tech for the black market, you Loth-Rat!' he shouted back to the dumbfounded pilot. With the helmet tucked under one arm, he sprinted across the field, heading for the hill that overlooked the area.

The pilot recovered fast. He flipped on the TIE's cannons and activated his targeting screen. Ezra was already scrambling up the hill as the pilot opened fire.

Reacting instantly to the sound of the blast, Ezra flipped sideways, dropping the helmet in the process. Laserfire exploded into the hill behind him. He rolled and came up standing with his energy slingshot raised at the TIE. But before he could let off a single stun-ball, the pilot fired again.

Ezra leapt high into the air, jumping over the laserfire, and the power of the blast hurled his body across the hill. He hit the ground and rapidly released two stun-balls, sending them straight at the TIE's fuselage. The stun-balls struck the fuselage without any effect.

Ezra let off a third stun-ball that travelled in a high arc towards the TIE. The stun-ball ricocheted off the back of the open canopy and slammed into the back of the pilot's head, instantly dazing him. The pilot collapsed facedown over his controls.

Dust was still settling around Ezra as he lowered his slingshot. 'Well, that was fun,' he said. He looked around and muttered, 'Now, where . . .'

He spotted the black helmet he'd dropped, went over to it, and picked it up. Inspecting it, he declared, 'This helmet is property of Ezra Bridger.' He shrugged. 'Or it is now, anyway.' He placed the helmet over his head. It was much too large for him. He pulled it off and held it at his side. Turning back to face the crashed TIE fighter, he raised his free hand to salute the unconscious pilot and said, 'Sir, thank you, sir!'

Ezra headed home, eager to add the helmet to his collection. But as he walked through the grassy plains of Lothal, he thought about this place he called home. People were always coming and going. Moreena had left with her family. Bossk came and went, and was probably off to start another dangerous adventure. Ezra wondered what else was ahead for him.

Then his mind went back to the diamond-shaped freighter that had not only evaded but brought down the TIE fighter. He wondered if he would ever find out who owned and operated the freighter, or what they had done to attract the TIE pilot's attention.

Although he'd seen many starships come and go over the years, he had a feeling he'd see that freighter again.